BOOKS BY J.E.B. SPRE...
(*J. Spredemann)

AMISH GIRLS SERIES

Joanna's Struggle
Danika's Journey
Chloe's Revelation
Susanna's Surprise
Annie's Decision
Abigail's Triumph
Brooke's Quest
Leah's Legacy

DISCARD

NOVELS*

*Love Impossible**
*Amish by Accident**
*An Unforgivable Secret** - *Amish Secrets 1*
*A Secret Encounter** - *Amish Secrets 2*
*A Secret of the Heart** - *Amish Secrets 3*
*An Undeniable Secret** - *Amish Secrets 4*
A Secret Sacrifice - *Amish Secrets 5*
*A Secret of the Soul** - *Amish Secrets 6*
Learning to Love – *Saul's Story** (Sequel to *Chloe's Revelation* – adult novella)
*Englisch on Purpose (*Prequel to *Amish by Accident)**

NOVELLAS

A Christmas of Mercy – Amish Girls Holiday
*Christmas in Paradise – (*Final book in *Amish by Accident*
trilogy)

NOVELETTES*

Cindy's Story – An Amish Fairly Tale Novelette 1*
Rosabelle's Story – An Amish Fairly Tale Novelette 2*

COMING 2018 (Lord Willing)

A Secret Christmas – Amish Secrets 2.5

Unofficial Glossary
of Pennsylvania Dutch Words

Ach – Oh

Aldi – Girlfriend

Alt Maedel – Old Maid

Bann – Shunning

Boppli – Baby

Bopplin – Babies

Buss – Kiss

Daed/Dat – Dad

Dawdi Haus – A small house intended to house parents or grandparents

Denki – Thanks

Der Herr – The Lord

Deitsch – Pennsylvania German

Dochder – Daughter

Englischer – A non-Amish person

Ferhoodled – Mixed up, crazy

Gott – God

Grossdawdi – Grandfather

Grossmammi – Grandmother

Gut – Good

Jah – Yes

Kapp – Amish head covering

Kinner – Children

Mamm – Mom

Mudder – Mother

Nee – No

Ordnung – Rules of the Amish community

Schatzi – Sweetheart

Sehr gut – Very good

Sohn – Son

Verboten – Forbidden

Was is less – What is wrong?

Characters in *A Secret of the Soul*

The Zook Family

Elam – Protagonist

Danny – Elam's Amish brother

Scramble – Elam's dog

The Zachariah Zook Family

Zach – Elam's ex-Amish cousin (Antagonist of *A Secret Sacrifice*)

Rosanna – Zach's ex-Amish wife (Protagonist of *A Secret Sacrifice*)

The Yoder Family

Julianna (Julie) Yoder – Elam's Amish ex-girlfriend

Obadiah Yoder – Julianna's father

Elnora Yoder – Julianna's mother

Mark Yoder – Julianna's brother

Naomi Yoder – Julianna's sister

Others

Martha Yoder – Julianna's cousin

Chase – Elam's *Englisch* friend from church

Mike – Elam's *Englisch* friend from church and leader of the singles class

Megan – A young *Englisch* woman who attends Elam's church

Tabitha Stolzfoos – Danny's girlfriend

Cletus Stolzfoos – Tabitha's older brother and Julianna's ex-boyfriend

Mose Hershberger – Amish bishop

To those who have selflessly cared for loved ones in their time of need. Take comfort in the words of Jesus, "Verily I say unto you, Inasmuch as ye have done it unto one of the least of these my brethren, ye have done it unto me."

Author's Note

It should be noted that the Amish/Mennonite people and their communities differ one from another. There are, in fact, no two Amish communities exactly alike. It is this premise on which this book is written. I have taken cautious steps to assure the authenticity of Amish practices and customs. Old Order Amish and New Order Amish may be portrayed in this work of fiction and may differ from some communities.

We, as *Englischers*, can learn a lot from the Plain People and their simple way of life. Their hard work, close-knit family life, and concern for others are to be applauded. As the Lord wills, may this special culture continue to be respected and remain so for many centuries to come, and may the light of God's salvation reach their hearts.

ONE

"You're joking, right?" Elam Zook reclined in the easy chair, and his eyes zeroed in on his cousin Zachariah. Although he admitted thinking about it a time or two himself over the past few years, the idea was preposterous.

"Why not? You're single and young. For the most part, anyway." Zach laughed.

Elam threw the wadded paper towel, from the snack they'd previously enjoyed, at his cousin. "Twenty-seven is hardly an old man."

"Not by *Englisch* standards, no. But by Amish standards you're practically unmarriable."

"There's plenty of men who have gotten married at my age or older." Why did he feel a need to defend himself?

"Name one," Zach challenged.

Elam wiped his hands on his jeans. "Okay. Uh…"

"See? I told you."

"*Ach*, give me a minute to think." His lips twisted. "Silas Bontrager."

"Doesn't count. He was a widower."

Elam frowned. "Doesn't count?"

"Nope. We're talking *single* men."

"I thought you were trying to talk me *in*to going back, not out of it."

"You missed my point. I didn't say to go back and make a kneeling confession. Just scope out the place. You know, ask around. See if…" Zach met Elam's gaze and a knowing look passed between them.

"See if Julianna Yoder is married?" His forehead creased. "Why not?"

"It's a ridiculous idea."

Zach nodded, a grin creeping up one side of his mouth. "What would it hurt? You have no clue how many times I've heard you speak her name, yet I've never met her. She must've meant *something* to you. Besides, you need to find yourself a good woman."

He ignored that last comment. He didn't *need* a woman. Did he? "Nah, I know she's married. She has to be."

"But you're not *sure*."

"As sweet and as beautiful as Julie was, there's no way she'd still be single."

"Are you afraid of what you might find?"

"Yes! Who knows which of my friends she's married to."

"Aren't you curious? What if she's *not* married? What then?"

"Exactly my point."

"You could save her from being an *alt maedel*."

"She's not. Trust me. There's no way. Besides, do you know how much she hurt me? I couldn't go through that again." He clutched his heart for effect.

"I thought you left because you wanted to become *Englisch*."

"Nope. She just sealed my decision to leave. I would have stayed if she hadn't..." Elam sighed. "I promised myself I wouldn't go back."

"O...kay."

"Okay, what? What's that supposed to mean?"

"At one time, I thought things were hopeless between Rosanna and me. Now look at us." His eyes narrowed and he pointed to his prosthetic leg. "And I'm not even a whole man."

Just then, Rosanna Keim, or Rosanna Zook for the past six years, entered the room with a little one in her arms. "I think she wants her daddy."

Elam didn't miss the look of love in her eyes as they made contact with her husband's.

"And you, Zachariah Zook, are all the man I want."

Zachariah took the baby from her arms and his features lit with joy. How could his cousin have a passel of children already, yet *he* didn't even have a wife? Or a girlfriend, for that matter. No one would ever call him lucky in love, that's for sure.

"I'm going to make supper now. Will you keep an eye on the children?"

Zach nodded, his gaze never leaving the little one in his arms.

"You'll need to check on Johnny, Lena, and Isaac. They're playing on the swings," Rosanna reminded, then planted a kiss on her husband's cheek. She turned to Elam. "You joining us for supper?"

"Nah. I better get home." He wasn't sure why he proffered an excuse. It wasn't like he had anything important to do at home. Nope. The only thing that awaited him at home were four square walls, and a decent size television with a handful of movies he'd already watched too many times.

And Scramble. He couldn't forget Scramble. His beloved mixed yellow lab had got him through many a lonesome day. But sometimes, humans just needed human companionship. Not the easiest thing to find for a former Amish man whose family and friends had all remained Amish.

At least he had Zach. He'd grown up in another district but they were cousins by blood. And both ex-Amish. Although *he* hadn't served in the military like his cousin had, he had been shunned because he'd become an official baptized member at the age of sixteen. He never thought at the time he'd come to regret that decision–he was fully committed to his people. But when the situation with Julianna transpired, he knew he couldn't stay.

If it wasn't for Zachariah and Rosanna and their encouragement, he'd probably still be Amish. And miserable. Now that he'd tasted freedom, he didn't see going back as a possibility. Ever.

Elam knew the idea of returning to his Amish community was preposterous, so why couldn't he get it out of his mind? Zachariah's words played in his head once again. *You could save her from becoming an alt maedel.* Even more preposterous was the idea of Julianna having not found a suitor after he'd left. *It's impossible.*

He had to find out for sure, didn't he? He'd thought he'd been sure. After he'd heard the rumors years ago, he'd wanted to go back but couldn't get himself to do it. But now…what if she *had* become an old maid? Of course, that wouldn't be his fault. She'd had her chance with him. So then why was he even considering going back?

Deep in his soul, he knew what it was. It was almost as if there were some unseen force compelling him onward. Was it the voice of God? He couldn't be for sure and certain. He just knew that if he *didn't* go, he wouldn't find peace.

TWO

Olam pulled his baseball cap down as far as it would go and adjusted his sunglasses. Hopefully, his thin goatee and *Englisch* clothing would brand him an *Englischer*. He'd have to remember his posture—no stooping as many of his people carried themselves. He needed to maintain the demeanor of an *Englischer*, shoulders straight and proud. He'd have to remember not to let his *Deitsch* accent slip. Since he'd left five years ago, that was one thing he'd tried desperately to lose. He only spoke in his mother tongue when he and Zach were out somewhere and wanted to keep their conversation between the two of them. But one's heritage was not something one could just lose at the drop of a hat, even if intentional.

Goosebumps prickled on his arms as his vehicle entered his former Amish community. As he passed each familiar house, remembrances of years gone by—the church meetings, youth singings, and those who occupied each home—had come rushing back like a locomotive hurling down the tracks at maximum speed. But one memory in particular jarred his thoughts. His final day with Julianna.

Over the years, he'd dated just a handful of girls in his Kentucky district. Most, only once. There were two who'd ever held a special place in his heart, or he'd thought he might have a chance with. The first was Saloma Troyer, who had come from Pennsylvania to work as a school teacher. They would have made a good match had her heart not already belonged to an *Englischer*. She and William Griffith were married less than a year later, probably with several children by now. At that time, he never would have considered becoming an *Englischer* himself. But time and circumstances had a way of changing things.

Then there was Julianna.

Elam was certain she was his one true love. They'd dated in secret for just over a year. He had every intention of marrying her. But when he approached her father and asked for her hand, he'd flat-out refused to let his daughter marry him. When asked why, her father hadn't given him a reason.

In his heart, he knew the reason. Her father hadn't thought him good enough for his daughter.

Because Elam's father had been injured in a buggy accident years prior, he hadn't been too successful with finances. Injuries were tough for Amish families who depended on physical labor for their income. The entire community knew that their family's funds had been lacking at times and they'd pitched in to help. When Elam was old enough, he'd found odd jobs working for *Englischers* and was able to contribute. But apparently, that hadn't been good enough for Julianna's father.

He knew he shouldn't have, but at the time, he'd asked Julianna to leave the community with him. He couldn't imagine not being married to her. But she refused to leave their people, and he knew she'd been scared. Now that he thought back on it, he wondered if she, too, had doubted his ability to provide for her.

The next thing Elam knew, Julianna was riding home from singings with Cletus Stolzfoos. Cletus just so happened to be from one the most well-respected and wealthiest families in their district. His father owned a five-hundred-acre spread including a prosperous horse ranch. Cletus' father had trained horses that went on to win the Kentucky Derby. Cletus appeared to be walking in his father's footsteps, and as the youngest son, stood to inherit the Stolzfoos property. They had no lack of material possessions, unlike Elam's family.

That was when Elam decided it would be best if he left. He couldn't bear to stick around and watch the woman he loved marry another and start a family with him. He couldn't bear attending meeting and other community-wide functions and seeing the love of his life ride home with another man. As he mused on it now, the thought still sickened him to his stomach.

According to the rumors, though, the relationship with Cletus hadn't lasted. Elam had already been in the world for six months then, making a good living, and he was still too upset to return home. Julianna had made her choice, and it wasn't him. He still sent his family money each month to help them get by—anonymously, of course, although he was quite certain his folks knew it was from him. *Mamm* hadn't wanted him to leave but he saw no other choice if he wanted to keep his sanity. He'd already lost his heart.

What am I even doing here?

He wasn't ready to do this yet.

He spun into the closest driveway to turn his truck around. He began backing up and a distinct *thud* grabbed his attention. His head whipped around to see a buggy toppled over on its side.

Oh no! I hit someone. Shoot!

He immediately pulled his vehicle forward into the driveway he'd just backed out of and shut off the engine. He ran around his truck to the buggy. He crouched down in front of the buggy's windshield, which seemed to be intact.

A woman lay on her side inside the buggy. He prayed she wasn't injured.

"Ma'am, are you all right?"

She seemed startled, and understandably so. "*Jah*, I'm *gut*. I think." She began to move.

Elam thrust forth his hand to stop her. "Wait. Don't move yet. Does anything hurt?"

"*Nee*. I'm fine. I might have a bruise or two, but I don't think anything's broken."

He pulled his cell phone from his pants pocket.

"What are you doing?"

"I'm going to call 9-1-1."

"*Nee*. No! I'm fine, really."

He understood her aversion to calling an ambulance. Most Amish in his district took care of issues on their own as much as possible, only procuring a doctor's care if absolutely necessary.

The horse whinnied.

"I need to get out," she insisted.

"Let me help." He examined the buggy for the best possible way to escape. "Can you crawl through the back?"

"I think so."

"Okay. If anything hurts too badly, I want you to stop. Okay?"

"*Jah*."

Elam looked up to see a buggy coming from the opposite direction. The driver pulled to the side of the road and two men jumped out and crossed the road. He recognized the older man, but not the younger one.

"Martha? Are you okay?" The younger man rushed to the woman.

"*Jah*, I'm fine." She'd managed to crawl out of the buggy and stood up. Her prayer *kapp* sat disheveled on her head.

Elam stepped forward. "I'm so sorry. I didn't even see you."

"Stupid *Englisch*."

He understood what the young man had spoken in their native language.

The young woman frowned. "*Nee*. It was an accident." She'd replied in the language they thought he couldn't understand.

"He was careless." The man shook his head. "*Dat* will be upset about his buggy."

They must be brother and sister. Maybe I should let them know somehow that I can understand them. But he didn't want to give away his identity.

The older man stroked the horse's head. He looked back at the buggy. "Help me get this upright. We'll need to try to unhitch the horse first. I think she's calm enough now." At least he'd spoken in English.

"What would you like for me to do?" Elam offered, pretending to be clueless, like the *Englischer* they presumed him to be.

They eyed him, most likely doubting he could be of any use at all.

The younger man grunted as a car pulled up.

"Why don't you direct traffic?" The older man suggested.

"Okay." Elam turned back to the young woman again. "I'm really sorry, miss."

He waved the car through and frowned when another buggy rolled up and stopped. Another man got out and crossed the road. This was becoming uncomfortable. He turned as though watching for traffic, hoping to not be recognized. He had no desire to let these people know his identity, yet he was thankful for the help.

He briefly wondered about Martha and her brother. He didn't think he'd ever seen them before, but something about Martha seemed familiar to him. Did they live in a neighboring Amish community?

In a short time, they had the buggy upright and the horse standing. By looking them over, both seemed to be in remarkably good condition. The buggy had a tear in the exterior vinyl and the wheel seemed like it might be slightly bent, nothing an Amish artificer couldn't repair. The horse's eyes were wide and she pranced anxiously, as though she were scared. But she didn't seem to be injured.

He now wondered if his auto insurance covered horse and buggy replacement, something he'd never considered in the past. He'd never been one to carry a lot of cash, and he knew he only had a couple of twenties in his wallet. Perhaps he should offer those. He pulled his wallet out and removed the bills.

"I don't know how much it'll take to fix your buggy, but I have some cash on hand. It's not much." He shrugged and offered it to the young woman.

She glanced toward her brother, who was now looking over the horse with the two other gentleman. She looked unsure whether she should accept the money or not.

"I could give you my number, or you could give me yours. I can call you after I talk to my insurance agent. I'm not sure whether they cover horse and buggy. If they don't, I'll pay whatever it costs to have the buggy repaired."

"Let me ask my brother, Jerome." She called the young man over and explained the situation in their native tongue.

The young man, Jerome, nodded and took the money from Elam's hand without saying a word.

"I'll get my number for you." Elam ran back to his truck for a pen and piece of paper. He scribbled down his number, tore the paper in half, and handed it to the young woman. "Will you write your number down?"

"We don't have a home phone, just the one in the phone shanty. You could leave a message." She began to write the number down, but her brother grabbed the pen from her and thrust it back at Elam.

"*Nee.* We will call you if we need to." It was obvious this young man didn't like him and was trying to be difficult.

Elam didn't protest and took his pen back. "Okay. Just let me know."

By the look of it, the older man agreed to drive the damaged buggy. The brother and sister made their way toward the other buggy the two men had originally arrived in.

"Wait! I don't know your name," Elam called out.

"Martha. Martha Yoder."

Yoder?

Elam watched as the two buggies drove away. Could it be that this Martha Yoder was related to Julianna? Yoder was a popular name, but it wasn't as common in these parts as it was in other Amish communities. There was a very real possibility that Martha and Julianna Yoder were related.

Was this just a coincidence, or had God allowed their paths to cross for a reason?

THREE

"Elam Zook."

Elam turned from the pew he was about to vacate and looked up at the possessor of the voice that had called for his attention. Ted Jorgenson, the assistant pastor, approached.

"Yes, Brother Ted?"

"Have you thought about joining our singles group? I'm certain you'd enjoy it."

"No, I haven't. When is it? And where?"

"They meet here at the church. Sometimes they just hang out here and have Bible study and fellowship. And other times they go out bowling, play volleyball, ice skating, or some other outdoor activity."

Hmm. Kind of sounds like an Amish singing.

"I'm not sure."

"It would give you a chance to get to know some of the young men and women your age. Singles from one of our sister churches also come from time to time."

"Is the purpose to find a mate?"

Ted chuckled. "Not specifically. But I can't say that some of our married couples haven't emerged from the singles group. Are you looking for a spouse?"

Now *that* was a question. *Was* he looking for a spouse? He wasn't sure himself.

"Not particularly. But if God brings one along, that's fine with me."

"Well, you never know what God might have planned for you." Ted cupped his shoulder. "The singles meet at six on Saturday evenings. I'm sure they wouldn't mind a new member joining their group."

Elam nodded. "No promises, but I'll think about it."

"Good. You do that. Will I see you at church Wednesday night?"

"I'll be there." He shook Ted's hand and watched him walk off to join his wife and children. The man seemed to be about five years older than Elam, but seemingly had his whole life together. Maybe he should consider going to this singles thing. What could it hurt? He could try it out once and if he didn't like it, he could stop going. No big deal.

"Hey, what was that all about?" Zach approached.

"Oh, Pastor Ted invited me to the singles group." He shrugged.

"You should go." Zach nodded. "Going to the Reformer's Unanimous meetings here at the church saved my life. I was stubborn about going at first, but after what happened with John…" He swallowed and his voice trailed off. "You should go."

Elam knew that speaking about Zach's former best friend stirred up too many emotions, but he already knew what his cousin hadn't said. Zach lived with many regrets—things in his past that were impossible to make right. It was something he'd learned to live with, but it hadn't been easy. Only his faith in God had sustained him.

"I might just do that." Elam smiled.

The last thing he wanted was to live with regrets. Which was why he needed to figure out some things. Namely, what Julianna was doing these days.

Elam grabbed a nail from his tool belt and hammered it into the window frame of the storage shed he was building. His mind had been wandering all day, it seemed. Truth be told, he was nervous about attending the singles gathering tonight.

For the most part, he considered himself slightly introverted. He didn't despise being around others, he just felt uncomfortable in a setting unfamiliar to him. And while he enjoyed getting to know people one on one, being the center of attention was not his thing. He appreciated peace and quiet, but he also liked having friendships, which was what he was hoping to find at the singles gathering.

Elam's lips twisted as he perused his closet. What on earth did people wear to these things anyway? Should he dress how he would for church on Sunday, in khakis and a button down? Somehow, that seemed too formal. He stood in front of his closet and grimaced.

This must be how females feel when getting dressed for an occasion. Not that he knew anything about that. But he'd heard Zachariah mention Rosanna a time or two. The Amish life was so much simpler. No closet full of clothes to decide from. He stood there another minute and decided a t-shirt would be too casual, so he finally grabbed a short-sleeved buttoned plaid shirt and a pair of dark jeans.

His palms now began to sweat as he contemplated getting out of the vehicle. *Sheesh!* It wasn't like he'd never met new people before. He looked on the seat at his Bible. Did he need to bring it along? Pastor Ted hadn't said it was a Bible study. Yet, it *was* a church activity. He would err on the side of caution.

"Elam?" a voice called as he emerged from his truck.

"Hey, Chase. I didn't know you attended the singles group." His mind was instantly set at ease as his friend approached and shook his hand.

"Oh, yeah. I wouldn't miss it. Glad you're here."

"Thanks. Me too."

They walked toward the building where Sunday school classes were typically held. Chase opened the door.

"Hey, guys." Mike Buller, another acquaintance from church, greeted them.

They both shook Mike's hand.

"Feel free to grab a few slices of pizza and a drink," Mike

offered. "Good to see you here, Brother Elam."

Elam smiled and nodded.

A few moments later, after others had arrived, Mike called the group over to a circle of chairs. "Bring your food and have a seat."

Elam sat next to Chase and placed his plate of pizza on top of his Bible.

"Let's begin with prayer." Mike bowed his head and prayed. "Amen."

Elam looked around the group—about eight people in attendance, not including Mike. Five young women and three men, himself included. Quite a bit smaller than he'd imagined. And nowhere near the size of an Amish singing. This would only make up one family.

"Has everyone met Elam?" Mike smiled. "Everyone this is Elam. Elam, this is everyone."

Elam chuckled. "Hi, everyone."

"If you haven't gotten a chance to meet him, be sure to say hello before you leave this evening." Mike rubbed his hands together. "Okay. Let's get started." He looked around at each person there. "What would you say is one of the biggest challenges of being single?"

A pretty blonde, whom Elam hadn't met yet, raised her hand. "Everyone asking when I'm going to get married and start a family."

The group laughed and nearly everyone nodded in agreement.

Mike looked at her. "How do you usually respond to that question, Megan?"

Now Elam knew her name.

"Well, I usually say something like 'when God brings the right person to me.'" She smiled and caught Elam's eye.

"And how do they respond to that?" Mike queried.

"They usually just nod. But it doesn't stop them from asking again."

Mike looked at the group again. "Anyone else?"

Chase spoke this time. "Staying pure. In thoughts and action."

"Ooh, that's a tough one." Mike nodded. "Anyone else?"

Another girl raised her hand. "It seems like everyone thinks that singleness is a curse or something. I mean, does everyone *have* to get married?"

"Great question, Amber." Mike opened his Bible. "Let's read what Paul has to say about that. Turn to First Corinthians chapter seven. Let's start with verse one and read through to nine." He proceeded to read the verses.

"I think this pretty much answers Amber's question, and the issues Chase brought up. Paul, who was single, by the way, writes that he desired that men and women remain unmarried so they can devote themselves to the Lord.

"So, to answer your question, Amber, no. There is absolutely nothing wrong with remaining single." He looked to Chase. "However, if you cannot keep yourselves pure, Paul recommends marriage. And there's absolutely nothing wrong with this either. Remember, God said in the Garden of Eden 'it is not good that man should be alone.'" Mike laughed. "God knows us men pretty well.

"I think the important part here is to bring God glory. And we can't do that if we're living in sin."

Everyone in the group nodded in agreement.

"Hi!"

Elam turned from the snack table and found Megan next to him. "Hello." He smiled.

"Elam, right?" She reached her hand forward and he shook it. "I'm Megan."

"Good to meet you, Megan."

"I'm glad you made it tonight. Will you come again?"

He shrugged. "I'm not certain. Probably, though."

"Good. Did you have a good time?"

"*Jah.* Yes."

"I think I've seen you in church a few times. I'm in the nursery or teaching Sunday school quite a bit, so I don't get a chance to mingle too much."

"You like children?"

She laughed and he wondered why. "Yes, I do. Do you?"

He shrugged. "Sure."

"So, are you from around here, Elam?"

He nodded. "Yeah. I was born in Ohio, but my folks moved down to Kentucky when I was about fifteen."

"How old are you now?"

"I'm twenty-seven. You?"

"Twenty-three." She smiled, and he thought her quite becoming.

Would it be proper to ask her out on a date? Or should he ask her brother? Did she even have a brother? He was unsure. He'd never dated an *Englischer*, so this was all unfamiliar territory.

"Well, it was nice meeting you, Elam." Megan looked at him and then back to the door where another young woman stood. "I think Hayley wants to go now. I hope to see you here next time."

"You, too." He watched as she walked toward the other girl and the two of them exited the building.

Chase joined him at the table. "Did you ask her out?"

"What?"

Chase smiled. "It's pretty obvious Megan likes you."

Elam frowned. "She does?"

"I've never seen her talk to any guy that long."

"That would be appropriate?"

"What? To ask her out? Why not?" He chuckled.

"I don't know. Do you think she would say yes?"

Chase clasped his shoulder. "There's only one way to find out, buddy."

FOUR

Elam hung up the phone. The insurance agent had suggested that he pay for the damage out-of-pocket since his deductible was five hundred dollars and the buggy repairs would most likely be less than that amount. And it would be preferable to reporting the incident and having it on his record.

But now he had a problem. He didn't have Martha Yoder's phone number and had no idea where she lived. Who knew how much the community had changed in the time he'd been gone. The only way to find out is to drive through Amish country again. This time, though, he'd take his motorcycle. And maybe, since he was looking for a Yoder, he'd stop by the ice cream shop to see if he could locate Martha and possibly learn something of Julianna's whereabouts. He just hoped he could remain undetected.

There appeared to be only one person manning the ice cream counter as Elam approached.

"I'd like one scoop of mint 'n chip and one of peanut butter and chocolate, please." He eyed the teen boy over the counter as he handed him the money. Could he possibly be Julie's younger brother, Mark? Her brother had been about ten when they dated. He mentally counted what his age would be now. Yes, it was possible.

"What happened to the Amish girl who used to work here?" He attempted to sound as casual as he could.

"Molly got hitched last year." He handed Elam the ice cream cone.

"Her name wasn't Molly. Julianna?"

He hated that he was trying to be deceitful, yet he couldn't let on that he had been Amish.

The boy frowned and studied him carefully. "Who wants to know?"

"I'm just curious. She was kind and always had a nice smile."

The boy smiled briefly but then it fell flat. "She's dead."

The revelation nearly knocked the wind out of him. *No! God, please don't let it be true. Please.* There were so many things he'd left unsaid. "What? But she... How?"

The boy shook his head, then walked toward the back of the shop. Apparently, that would be all he would get out of him. But it was enough, wasn't it? If Julianna was gone, little else mattered.

Elam took a piece of paper from his pocket, remembering

his other reason for coming. "Excuse me. Do you know where I can find this person?"

"Why do you ask?" He eyed him suspiciously.

"I hit her buggy with my truck the other day and I contacted my insurance company. I need to discuss what they said with her." Surely, the whole community had already heard about the buggy accident. News like that traveled faster than any newspaper in their community.

The young man nodded. "My cousin Martha. Lives down in the holler off Milton Ridge Road. Third house. Can't miss it."

"Milton Ridge Road. Okay, thank you for your help." Elam smiled and left a dollar and a Gospel tract on the counter. "A tip for you." He nodded and walked back out to his motorcycle.

He looked at his cone, only half eaten, and decided he should have only gotten one scoop. He leaned against the bike and thought about what Julianna's brother had said about her. As sadness filled him once again, he no longer felt like finishing his ice cream cone.

A million questions filled his mind. Questions he had to find the answers to, but had no clue how to go about getting them without revealing his identity. But if he did reveal his identity, the answers would be closed off for sure.

How did Julianna die? When did she die? Was she married? Who did she marry? Did she die giving birth? Did she leave a family behind? How old was she?

Maybe, if he played his cards right, he could possibly get answers from Martha. Surely she knew what had befallen her cousin. He had to think of a way he could get her alone. But how?

Elam veered right and turned into what he presumed to be the Yoder family's driveway. The house and barn certainly wouldn't be mistaken for the grandest home in the Amish community. However, it seemed clean and tasteful.

He immediately noticed a young woman hanging out clothes on the line beside the house. It looked like it could be Martha. As soon as he stopped the motorcycle and dismounted, she began heading to the house, most likely to inform a male member of the household so he could speak with him. If only he could catch her before she went inside.

He quickly replaced his motorcycle helmet with his ball cap.

"Martha," he called out.

She turned and he waved, hoping she'd recognize him. She stopped, as though contemplating what to do.

"I got ahold of my insurance company from the buggy accident." He took a few steps closer.

She nodded and proceeded to walk toward the house.

"Wait. May I speak with you?"

She looked back toward the house, then looked at him,

probably to determine whether he was harmless or not. She nodded again and began walking toward him.

Would she be scared off if he began talking about Julianna right away? He had to chance it before another member of the Yoder family joined them.

"Are you related to Julianna Yoder?"

Her eyes immediately flew wide.

"I was a friend. Her brother told me that she passed away."

She nodded. "*Jah.*"

Her confirmation sent another arrow through his heart and he frowned. "Do you know who she was married to?"

"*Nee.* She is…*was* not married."

"She wasn't? Really? I thought for sure… When did she die?"

"Nearly two years ago."

"How?"

She seemed uncomfortable, but he had to press on. He needed to get as much information as he could.

She frowned, obviously ill at ease with this conversation. "Uh, sickness."

"I'm sorry to hear that. Her folks, do they still live in the same place?"

"*Jah.*"

A young man descended the steps and began walking in their direction.

"Listen, Martha. I would appreciate it if you didn't say anything to anyone about our conversation." His tone was low.

She nodded.

"May I help you?" The young man approached. This man seemed a little older than the one who'd been at the scene of the accident.

"Yes. I was in the accident with Martha here." He looked to her and lifted a half smile. "I was just telling her that I spoke with my insurance company. Did you have the buggy repaired?"

"*Jah*. Just yesterday."

"Do you have a receipt for how much it cost?"

"*Nee*. My father fixed it. Probably cost him less than a hundred." He shrugged.

Elam fished his wallet out of his pocket and handed him two hundred dollar bills. "Please give him this for parts and labor. Will you see that he gets it?"

The man smiled ever so slightly and nodded.

"Thank you. Good day." He tipped his baseball cap at them and shared a knowing glance with Martha before hopping back on his motorcycle.

"Sorry again, about the accident." He waved, put his helmet on, and then started the engine and headed down the road.

FIVE

or the second time that week, there Elam was out at Zach's ranch, searching for answers. He couldn't sleep last night with the heartbreaking information he'd received from Julianna's brother and Martha churning in his mind.

He had a hard time believing the truth of the situation. He could accept it if Julianna had moved on and gotten married, or moved away even. But *dead*? No. She *couldn't* be dead. His heart refused to believe it.

He'd lain awake thinking of all the things he would have said to her—should have said to her—had she still been alive. And Zach's prediction, as ridiculous as the notion was, had been correct—she hadn't been married. That was the kicker. How on earth could she have remained single?

When they'd courted, he was sure they'd had something that was real. Something that was true. Something that would last a lifetime. There was no doubt in *his* mind whatsoever. So when that fateful day came, the day they broke up, it had come as a complete shock to him.

At the time, he'd said things to her that he wished he could take back now. But there wouldn't be any taking back of anything. Julianna had died believing the words he'd spoken to her. Words that had stemmed from the hurt in his heart. Words that weren't even true. Why had he uttered them at all? Why had he waited to go back until it was too late?

This news of her death dug up old wounds that refused to be healed. If only he could have another chance. But he knew another chance was an impossibility.

What pained his heart the most now, was her eternal destiny. Did she ever come to know Jesus as her Saviour or did she die in her sins? If she was like most in their community, she'd been putting her stock into the fact that she was Amish, and doing her best to be a good person. They had never been taught that salvation was a free gift that could not be earned. Why hadn't he attempted to go back sooner and talk to her about it?

It was something he would, no doubt, regret his entire life. *I'm sorry, Julie. I'm truly sorry.*

Elam locked eyes with Zachariah. "I went back."

"And?" His expression was one of anticipation.

He couldn't help the moisture that pricked his eyes, no matter how hard he tried to suppress it. "She's gone, Zach."

"Gone?" Zach frowned.

He nodded. "Julianna is dead."

Zach's jaw dropped. "Are you serious?"

"I'm dead serious."

Zach shook his head. "That wasn't funny."

"I'm not trying to be funny."

"I'm really sorry, man." He clasped his shoulder.

"Why didn't I go back sooner?"

"I don't know. You weren't ready, I guess."

"I feel so helpless. I want to do something. I want to hold her close one last time. Apologize." He felt like an idiot, crying in Zach's presence but he couldn't stop his tears. He'd loved Julianna with everything in him.

"It's tough. Believe me, I know. I felt the same way when John died. He was gone and I felt responsible for his death. There was no way I could go back and thank him for all he'd done for me. I owe him my life."

"I know he was a good friend to you."

"The best." Zach shook his head. "And now, I have Rosanna and our children, and I'm raising John's son. It's unbelievable that God would find me worthy of any of these blessings. But I realized that it's not about my worthiness. It's about His goodness. His grace."

"The worst part about it is that I don't even know if Julie was saved." His heart squeezed tight at just the mention of it.

"That's hard, man. But there's not a single thing you can do to change the past. You have to move forward."

Elam dropped his head into his hands. "I know."

"God is going to somehow work this out for the good. You have His Word on it."

He looked at his cousin. "Thank you. I really needed that word of encouragement."

"Anytime." Zachariah shook his head. "I know this might not be the best time to say this, cousin, but I think you need to hear it."

Elam shrugged and took a deep shuttering breath. "Go ahead, I can take it."

"You need to find someone else. Someone that you can invest your time and your money in, and someone to care for."

"I thought that's what Scramble was for," Elam chuckled.

Zach tossed a menacing look at Elam. "You're helpless, you know that?"

"Do you think I should spend more time with the guys at the Y?"

"You could. But I was thinking more along the lines of a girlfriend."

"A girlfriend? Where on earth would I find a girlfriend?" An image of pretty Megan flitted through his mind.

"Why don't you pray about it?"

"Pray about it, huh?" Elam shrugged. "I guess I can do that."

Elam woke up refreshed the next day, after having given his worries to God. There was a good chance he'd never get the answers to all the unknown questions zigzagging through his head, and that was something he'd have to come to terms with. Fretting about something he couldn't change was fruitless.

He would attempt to move forward, as Zachariah had suggested. He couldn't do anything about Julianna, so he determined to move on with his life—as difficult as it was. And that meant trying to forget about her.

"Well, what do you think, Scramble?" Elam looked down at his dog, who cocked his head.

"Julie's not coming back. Zach was right. There's nothing I can do about it now. I need to move on."

Scramble licked Elam's hand. "Okay, go get it, boy!" He threw the tennis ball and the dog raced to the fence.

Scramble brought the ball back and dropped it at Elam's feet. "So, was that a yes? Should I ask Megan out?"

Scramble whined and tilted his head.

"Never mind, Scramble. Fetch." He tossed the ball again and mumbled to himself. "I really need to talk to a human." Because, while dogs were great companions, they gave lousy dating advice.

SIX

"Elam's thinking of asking Megan out." Zach's amused expression met his wife.

"Oh, she's sweet. I've talked to her in the nursery many times. I think you two would make a cute couple." Rosanna smiled.

"You do?" Elam looked at Zach's wife.

"Yes, I do. Did you talk to her father?" Rosanna bounced the baby on her hip.

"Her father?"

"Yes, Brother Hal." Zach nodded.

"I didn't know she was the deacon's daughter." He frowned. "So, I'm supposed to ask *him* first?"

Zach laughed. "You look petrified. I actually have no idea how the *Englisch* do dating, but this looks like it's gonna be fun to watch."

"Thanks for your help, man," Elam said wryly.

Zach chuckled. "Anytime."

"Now that I think about it, Chase said something about

asking her out." Elam shifted in his seat attempting to psychoanalyze what exactly Chase meant by his suggestion.

"That could present a problem." Zach cocked a brow. "So, Chase wants to date her too?"

"No, *I* do. I think." Elam chuckled nervously. What did he know about how the *Englisch* dated? *Nothing, that's what.*

"Well, I'm sure it wouldn't hurt getting to know her." Rosanna chimed in. "As far as I know, she's not seeing anyone."

"You might not want to wait too long, Elam. If she's a fine catch, chances are, you're not the only one with your pole in the pond."

"What?"

"Just ask her out."

Elam swallowed the knot in his throat. "Okay."

Elam tapped his fingers on his trousers as he waited for Megan to exit the sanctuary. He leaned against his vehicle and took a deep breath, soaking in the early afternoon rays and attempting to calm his nerves. He'd purposely parked next to Megan's car, a Volkswagen Beetle that he thought suited her perfectly. It was cute and little, just like its owner. And parked next to his beefy truck, the car seemed even more petite.

Megan's smile met his as she strolled toward her vehicle, purse and Bible in hand.

"Hi, Elam."

"Hi." This was his chance. It was now or never. "Are you, uh, do you want to go out?"

Her face brightened even more. "For lunch?"

He nodded. Did he have cotton stuck in his throat?

"Oh, I'm sorry. I have a casserole in the oven at home." She grimaced.

Not interested.

Elam shrugged, trying to attempt nonchalance and hide his disappointment. "That's okay. I understand." Was she just making an excuse?

"Would you like to join me?" *Apparently not.*

"For lunch today?" As if eavesdropping on their conversation, his stomach growled.

Megan laughed. "Was that a yes?"

"Apparently so." He rubbed his stomach. "I can't argue with that."

"If you're coming back to church tonight, you can leave your truck here and we can just take my car. Unless you have plans after lunch."

Elam smiled. "No. No plans. I'll leave my Bible in my truck and grab it when we return."

"Okay." She unlocked the door. Elam slid into the passenger's seat and felt around for a lever or button to extend the distance between himself and the dashboard. "Cute car. It suits you well."

Megan smiled. "Thanks. My dad says the same thing."

"Will your folks be there?"

"Do you mean for lunch?"

He nodded.

"No, they usually go out somewhere. On a typical Sunday, it's Cracker Barrel."

"I like Cracker Barrel. It has a nice old-fashioned feel to it."

Megan nodded. "Do you have a favorite thing to eat there?"

"Probably their chicken 'n dumplings with fried okra." His mouth was beginning to water just thinking about it. "What's yours?"

She signaled and turned onto a street. "I like the lemon pepper trout with cornbread muffins."

"Ah, I love their muffins! Although, I can't say I've tried their fish. I go fishing often so I usually order something else when I go out."

"I love fish. It's my favorite type of meat."

"Mine too." He grinned.

She pulled into a driveway. "Well, here we are. Home sweet home."

He looked up at the quaint home, which was situated in a modest neighborhood. For some reason, he'd expected the deacon to live in someplace fancier.

Megan pressed the beep for her alarm then led the way to the front door. Potted flowers on each side brought life to the otherwise plain entryway.

"Did you grow up in this home?"

"Here? No, I'm just renting." She turned the key and walked inside.

He frowned. Did she rent from her folks? He wasn't quite sure how the *Englisch* did things, so as far as he was concerned, anything was possible. "What time will your folks be coming home?"

"Here?" She laughed. "They're not planning to visit today."

"You live here alone?" His brow shot up. He noticed the faint lingering scent of perfume or a vanilla candle. He inhaled again, enjoying the scent.

"Not if you count Feathers."

"You have a bird?" He looked around for a cage.

Megan laughed. "No, Feathers is my cat. She likes to *eat* birds. The first time she showed up on my doorstep she had a feather in her mouth." She shrugged. "The name just stuck."

"It's a good name."

She entered a modest dining nook and gestured toward a small round table with four chairs. The kitchen was connected to it on one side, and a sliding glass door that led to a patio and backyard bordered the other side. "You may have a seat. I'm just going to check the casserole and set the table."

"I can help."

"Oh, no. It won't take but a minute." In no time, she set a clear square glass dish on the table with two hot pads.

"Mm…it smells good."

She returned again with a spatula, silverware, and two turquoise plates. "Would you like tea or water?"

"Tea would be nice. Thanks."

She set down a pitcher of tea and two glasses that matched the plates on the table. She sat down across from him. "Would you like to say the blessing?"

He nodded, then bowed his head in silence and gave thanks for the meal and the company. He cleared his throat and lifted his head.

Megan's head was still bowed.

"Amen," he finally said.

"Oh. I didn't know you had prayed. I was still waiting." She laughed.

"It was a silent prayer."

She reached for his glass and poured tea into it. "Is that how you always pray?"

"*Jah.*" He took a drink of his tea. It was unsweetened, he quickly discovered.

"Would you like some sweetener for that?"

"Uh, yeah. That would be nice."

She brought a bottle of something and salt and pepper shakers. "You might need those. When I'm just cooking for myself, I usually go light on the seasonings." She offered him the spatula and he helped himself to the casserole.

The aroma from the food tantalized his taste buds and he quickly dug in. The flavors were appetizing but it did, indeed, need salt. "It's *gut.*"

"Goot?" She laughed.

"Sorry, my *Deitsch* tends to slip from time to time."

"So, you're German then?"

"Amish."

Her brow shot up. "Amish?"

He never knew what kind of reaction he would get when he revealed that detail of his life to *Englischers*. "I *used* to be Amish. I left five years ago."

"Really? Wow, that must have been quite a culture shock for you."

He didn't particularly wish to discuss himself or the Amish. "Yeah. It was." He raised his fork. "This is really good. What is it?"

"Oh, it's a new recipe. This is only the second time I've tried it. It's lasagna, but instead of noodles, I used thinly sliced zucchini. I wanted to make it healthier."

"I didn't even notice. And I don't even care much for zucchini. But I like this."

"Oh, really? I love zucchini. It's such a versatile vegetable." She smiled. "As a matter of fact, I bought this from one of the Amish farms in the country."

"We used to grow a lot of zucchini. That's probably why I grew tired of it."

"That would be funny if I purchased this from one of your relatives."

"You may have." His gaze roamed around the cozy little house and took in his surroundings. From where he sat, he could see a small living room area with a couch, a chair, and a modest entertainment center, and a hallway that he guessed probably led to a bedroom or two and bathroom.

She must've noticed his eyes wandering. "I'll give you the grand tour when we're done."

"What do you do for a living?"

"I'm a teacher of sorts."

"Of sorts?"

"Yeah. I mostly work from my home. That's why you see that stack of papers there on my counter. I'm not the neatest person."

"It's clean compared to my place." Although he had been attempting to keep it cleaner as of late. His *mamm* would be appalled.

"I teach a small cooking class here twice a week. And dance on Friday evenings."

"Dance?"

"Ballroom Dancing. A bit eccentric to most people, I know. But I love it." She smiled. "Do you dance?"

He nearly choked on his tea. "No. I've never danced."

"You should try it sometime. It's fun."

"This is allowed?"

"Allowed? What do you mean?"

"By the bishop, or pastor, I mean."

"Well, typically, the pastor doesn't tell us what we may or may not do. He lets the Word of God speak to hearts, the way only the Holy Spirit can. I feel like there's nothing wrong with it, so long as I'm not dancing with another woman's husband. Most people who take my classes are married couples who enjoy it for the exercise or young engaged couples wanting to learn to dance for their wedding."

"What *is* ball room dancing exactly?" He guessed it had something to do with dancing in a room full of balls. Maybe like those children's playgrounds? But it seemed like it might be difficult to dance with a bunch of balls all around you. The absurdities of the *Englisch* culture never ceased to amaze him.

"There are several dances classified as ballroom, but I only teach a few different styles in my class. I would say the waltz and the tango are probably the most popular of the dances. With swing next in line." She must've noticed his blank stare. "I just spoke a foreign language to you, didn't I?"

He smiled and nodded.

"How about I show you later?"

He nodded. "Where?"

"When the weather is nice, I usually teach out on my patio. I have a tile dance floor that I had someone make for me. When the weather is not so nice, I usually use my garage or living room. The living room isn't so great because of the carpet and the dance floor doesn't fit, so I try to avoid it."

He frowned and looked around. "Where do you keep the balls when you're not dancing?" Perhaps they were out in the garage.

"Balls?"

"Yes, for dancing."

A puzzled look stretched across Megan's face.

"Ball room dancing."

"Oh, no." She burst into laughter. "You thought…" She doubled over and he began laughing too, although he wasn't quite sure what was so funny.

It took a full couple of minutes before she regained her composure. When she finally explained what a ballroom was, they both erupted in laughter once again.

Elam couldn't remember a time in his life that he'd ever laughed so much. It felt good.

"Oh, my." She wiped tears off her face and took a deep breath. "I guess I could see how you would think that."

"I was thinking maybe people danced around a bunch of balls like in the children's playground, or maybe those ones they use at the gym."

She laughed again. "Nope. No balls involved."

"I guess it would be difficult to maneuver around all those balls. I tried picturing it in my head and it just seemed strange to me."

"Well, now you know." She rose from the table and took their plates to the sink. "Would you like more tea?"

"Yes, please."

She poured more into his glass and filled her own as well, before putting the pitcher into the fridge.

"Would you like help with the dishes?" At home, he

would wait until Monday to wash the dishes. He tried to rest on the Lord's Day. That was one tradition from his Amish culture that he'd kept, because he thought it was fitting to set aside a day to focus on the things of God and rest.

"Oh, no, that's okay. I'm just going to let them soak right now. I'll do them tonight after I get home from church." She placed the remaining food in the refrigerator as well and quickly wiped the table down. "Are you ready for your tour now?"

"Sure." He rose from the table and followed her lead.

"It's not going to be all that long."

He smiled. "I figured as much."

"Living room." She gestured.

"It's cozy."

"I like it. It's just me so I don't need anything big. A whole house is enough to keep clean, even if it is small."

He nodded.

"Do you live alone?"

"I have a dog. His name is Scramble."

"Where did he get his name from?"

"I'm not sure. That was his name before I bought him."

"Did you ask the owners what it meant?"

"No. I had a friend buy it from an Amish farm for me."

"You didn't pick him out yourself?"

"Things can be complicated where I come from. They wouldn't have been allowed to sell it to me because I am shunned."

"Really? So, if an Amish family owns a store, you can't go in there and buy their merchandise?"

"They would allow me to come into the store, but they cannot accept my money. And they would probably ask me not to return to the store again."

"Isn't that a little harsh?"

He shrugged. "Those are the ways of my people. I guess it seems harsh to the *Englisch*, but that is what is to be expected if you leave. They think I am in danger of Hell because I left. I have received letters from family stating as much."

"So, they believe you have to be Amish to go to Heaven?"

"For me, yes. But for someone like you, they figure that you don't know any better so God might judge you differently."

"That's sad that they think that. So, do they believe in Jesus?" She now walked down a short hallway.

"They believe with their head, but not so much with their heart. They don't have a personal relationship with our Saviour." He frowned. "This was never taught to us. God was seen more as a judge than a friend."

"If I stopped by an Amish business and left a Gospel tract, would they accept it and read it?"

"Some probably would."

She smiled. "It looks like I just found a new mission field. Are they open to discussing Bible issues?"

"They might be. But many have very limited knowledge

of the Bible so it may make them uncomfortable."

Megan nodded to a bedroom. "Well, the rest of the house isn't much to brag about. Just my bedroom and a small office. The bathroom's through that door right there."

He peeked into each room and thought they were tastefully decorated, not that he was anywhere near an expert. He snickered at the thought.

"Shall we go outside?" Megan began walking down the hall, oblivious to Elam's musings.

"Sure."

More than one head turned to look when they arrived back at the church together in Megan's car. Elam quickly retrieved his Bible from his truck, then joined her as she walked to the entrance.

"I enjoyed lunch. Thanks for inviting me over."

"Anytime. I had a nice time too, Elam." Megan smiled. "Next time, we'll have to try those dance lessons I mentioned."

Next time? That sounded promising.

Elam grimaced. "I'm giving you fair warning. I'm not going to be all that great at it and you might get your toes stepped on."

Megan laughed. "Oh, they've been stepped on plenty of times. That doesn't bother me. I think anyone can dance if they want to."

"No, not anyone." He frowned, thinking of his cousin Zach's missing leg.

"I once had a man in a wheelchair who danced with his wife. It was a bit different, but they learned to dance beautifully together."

"Can you teach someone with a prosthesis?"

She shrugged and smiled. "I don't see why not. It may be more challenging, but I find that many times the more challenging it is, the more rewarding success is."

"Hmm... something to think about." He opened the door to the church. "Shall we?"

"Sure. Where would you like to sit?"

She's going to sit with me? If people hadn't noticed them driving up or walking in together, they surely would notice them now. He picked a spot near the middle. "Is this fine?"

"Good as any." They sat at the end of one of the pews.

"Your father won't mind?" He gulped as he saw the subject of conversation walking in their direction. His countenance unreadable.

She shrugged. "I don't think so."

They both stood as her father approached and offered his hand. "Elam, good to see you here this evening."

He shook his hand. "You too, Brother Hal."

A look passed between the deacon and his daughter, and she answered his unspoken question. "Elam joined me for lunch today."

Her father nodded but Elam was unsure if it equated to approval.

She had most likely only answered *one* of the many questions in his head. Elam wondered if he should mention his intentions.

"I asked Megan if she'd like to go out. Since she already had something cooking for lunch, she offered to share it with me."

Brother Hal smiled at his daughter. "I have no doubt it was delicious."

"Dad!" She playfully slapped his arm.

"Hey, I'm only speaking the truth. You can't help but be a great cook. You learned from the best." He winked.

Elam broke in. "It was very good."

The music to "I'll Fly Away" began playing and congregants began making their way to their seats.

"It looks like I'd better take my seat. I'll talk to you two more after the service."

SEVEN

Elam opened the door to his back patio and his dog rushed over to meet him, nearly knocking him down in his anticipation. "Okay, Scramble, let's get some exercise. You've been cooped up in that backyard all day. What do you say?"

Scramble cocked his head and whined in typical fashion, his eyes expectant. His delight evident by his wagging tale as Elam scratched his head and his chest.

"You want to go play catch at the school? Go get your ball."

Scramble raced off and retrieved his tennis ball from under a bush.

"Good dog." He took the ball and stuffed it into his pants pocket, and then clipped Scramble's leash to his collar. "Come on, boy. Let's go have some fun."

An hour later, Elam headed for home with a satisfied Scramble. He barely noticed as a vehicle pulled up beside him.

"Hey, stranger. You up for some dinner?"

Elam's grin widened and he slowed his step to keep pace with her Beetle. "Megan. I didn't expect to see you out this way. Scramble and I were just heading home."

Her car slowly moved beside him as they spoke. "So this is your dog. He's cute."

"Yeah, he's a good dog." He scratched his head. "You said dinner?"

"Yes. Have you eaten?"

"No, not yet."

"Oh, good. I'm not too late, then." Her smile made his stomach do a flip. "I brought something for us."

"Really?" His brow shot up. "Hey, how did you know I lived out this way?"

Megan grinned. "Google is a girl's best friend."

"Gotcha." He winked. "So, what'd you make?"

"You mentioned you like chicken and dumplings the other day, so I thought I'd make them. I'm not sure they're as good as Cracker Barrel's though."

"You made chicken 'n dumplings for me?" *How thoughtful.*

"I hope that's not too forward of me."

"Oh, no. It's wonderful! I just didn't expect it, is all. It's a nice surprise."

She released a relieved sigh. "Oh, good." She pulled up in front of his house at last.

He glanced down at his basketball shorts and t-shirt, both partially drenched with perspiration. "I hope you don't mind. I'm going to need a shower before I sit down to eat."

"Well, you don't have to on account of me."

"Trust me. I'll enjoy the food much better after a shower, and you'll enjoy the company better." He laughed and gestured for her to enter. "Enter at your own risk. I didn't expect company, as you'll soon discover."

"That's not a problem. You saw my place. I hadn't been expecting company either. I'll just snoop around your house while you're in the shower." He deduced by her smile that she was teasing.

"Be my guest. I have nothing to hide."

Her brow quirked up. "Nothing?"

He shook his head.

"I thought everybody had something to hide." Her eyes danced in curiosity.

Elam found himself being reeled in by her warm caramel gaze. Each time he saw her, his attraction seemed to grow. "If I think of something, I'll be sure *not* to let you know," he jested.

The shower felt great, although he was certain he finished in record time. He didn't want to leave Megan alone for too long, although she'd promised to keep herself busy setting the table. The food was in a slow cooker, so she hadn't needed to warm it up. His mouth watered just thinking about it.

He walked toward the dining room, where Megan was just filling two glasses with water.

"Wow! You clean up nice."

Her words brought a rush of heat to his ears. He looked down at his jeans and t-shirt, his typical post-shower attire. "Thanks."

"Wet hair looks *really* good on you, I must say."

He'd attempted to towel dry his hair, but apparently he hadn't done a good job. "*Ach*, I should have combed it."

"Oh, no. Not everyone can wear the messed up look, but you *definitely* can." Was she flirting with him?

"I can?"

"Yes." She smiled and gestured toward the table. "You hungry?"

He eyed the meal she'd prepared. Not just chicken and dumplings, but corn bread muffins and fried okra too. This woman was amazing. "Starving. Everything looks great."

"Would you like to pray?"

"Out loud?"

She nodded.

"I can, but I'm not sure if it will come out right. When I pray, it's usually in Pennsylvania Dutch. I can try in English, though."

"Have you never prayed in English?"

All of a sudden, he felt nervous about praying. "No. Never. So don't laugh."

"I wouldn't think of it."

"Okay." He bowed his head and clasped his hands in his lap. "God, thank you for Megan bringing this food over. Please bless it and use our hands to serve you." He looked up and realized she was waiting for him to continue. "Uh, amen."

Her head lifted and she smiled.

"I'm not sure that came out right."

"It was perfect." She offered Elam the serving spoon. "Dig in."

He did as suggested and helped himself to a decent helping of each dish, allowing her to do the same. When he took a bite of the chicken and dumplings, the flavor exploded in his mouth.

She watched him eat, but didn't touch her own. It seemed Megan couldn't enjoy her food properly if her guests weren't satisfied. Her gaze was expectant.

"It's delicious. Really." He took a forkful of the fried okra, then bit into his cornbread muffin.

Megan finally took a bite of her dinner as well. She shrugged. "I guess it's pretty good."

Elam shook his head. "No, it's better than pretty good. Cracker Barrel is lucky you don't have a restaurant next to them, otherwise you'd steal all their customers."

Megan's smile stretched wide across her face. "Okay, that's a bit of a stretch. I don't think Cracker Barrel's customers are going anywhere." She laughed.

Elam's heart gladdened to see her happy while in his company. "I mean it. You are a wonderful cook." He chuckled. "I'd belch to prove it, but Rosanna Zook informed me that's not a proper thing to do among the *Englisch.*"

"Oh, is that what you'd do at home in your Amish community?" She laughed.

"Yep. And if anyone ever said anything, we'd reply, '*It ain't bad manners, just good eatin'!*'" He laughed, recalling the memory.

"And your mother didn't mind?"

He shrugged. "Not that I know of. *Daed* did it all the time. Still does, as far as I know."

"It's interesting how different cultures determine what's acceptable social behavior and what's not."

"Yeah, when you're used to doing things a certain way and then you jump into another culture, it's almost like living in a whole nother world. It can be quite shocking. Could *you* imagine becoming Amish?"

"No, not at all. I mean, I'm sure I could if I was forced to but I would never join willingly."

"I totally understand. If I ever went back, I think it would be really difficult. Yet, at the same time, I would regain some things that I've lost. Like sharing a meal with my family."

"So, you're not even allowed to share a meal with them?"

"If I still lived under their roof as a shunned man, I'd have to eat at a separate table apart from the family."

"So, it would be like you're in 'timeout'?"

His brow shot up. "Timeout?"

"When children misbehave or disobey, a lot of parents put their children in 'timeout.' They have to sit alone by themselves and they don't get to play with the other children for a certain period of time."

"I believe in disciplining children when they disobey. If I didn't obey my *daed*, I got a spanking. I thought twice about disobeying the next time because I didn't like having a sore bottom. I couldn't imagine a 'timeout' would have persuaded me to obey. It just doesn't have the same motivational force. You know what I mean?" He laughed.

"Yeah, we got spanked too. But when I watch the children in nursery, I'm not allowed to spank someone else's child. 'Timeout' is our only option or we could call the parents in and have them take care of their child."

"Yeah, I guess eating alone would be similar to a 'timeout' then." He shrugged. "But since I've left, I don't even enjoy that privilege. When I visit, they meet me at the door and we talk outside."

Her eyes widened. "Oh my goodness, are you serious? I had no idea the Amish were that strict."

"Oh, they're not all like that. Each community lives by their own rules and standards, often passed down from previous generations. As a matter of fact, there's one district I know of where the Amish father lives with the shunned daughter and son-in-law. I don't think they even have any restrictions as far as eating together or not receiving money from the shunned member's hand—none of that. You probably wouldn't even know they were shunned unless someone pointed it out."

"Then what would the purpose of the shunning be?"

"Beats me. But I sure would like to have that kind of shunning." He looked down at his food that was most likely cold by now. "We should probably finish our supper, yeah?"

Megan laughed. "Probably. Would you like me to warm that up for you again?"

"No, thanks. I'm sure it's just as good either way." He smiled and dug into the remainder of his meal.

It was still delicious, but his mind wandered back to his folks' home. Back to a time when they would all sit together and share a meal. Back to when life had been devoid of the strife his shunning had caused.

If only things could've been different.

EIGHT

"Okay. The food is put away and the dishes are done. Time for your dance lesson." Megan grinned.

Elam swallowed. "Dance lesson?"

"Yes. Remember I told you that I teach dance?"

"Ah, yes, dancing with the balls."

Megan laughed, but corrected him. "Ballroom dancing." She looked around, no doubt surveying his house for a suitable dance floor. "I think your living room will do."

"I'm not sure about this."

"Elam, there's no need to be nervous. You'll do just fine." She waved him over to where she stood in the middle of his living room. Thankfully, it was a decent size for his small house. "Come on."

Apparently, there was no way of getting out of this without hurting her feelings, and that was the last thing he desired to do. He reluctantly joined Megan on the 'dance floor.'

"Okay. First of all, I want you to take a deep breath and

relax. Have a seat." She smiled and waited for him to do as told.

He watched as she transformed into teacher mode, slowly pacing back and forth in front of him. "Now, dancing is a lot like a marriage. The man leads, while keeping in time with the music, and the woman follows. If any of these parts are neglected or not taken seriously, the dance becomes awkward and off-beat. It's not beautiful anymore, the way it was intended to be. However, if the man listens to the music—I liken the music to God—and follows the direction of the music, then he will lead his partner with confidence and they won't misstep. When the woman follows his confident leadership, the couple will glide across the floor in elegance. This brings honor to the song and to those dancing to it."

Elam smiled, enjoying Megan's explanation. He hadn't expected to get a spiritual lesson along with his dance lesson.

"Before we begin, I want to go over your part so that you know what to do." Her eyes met his. "Now watch me because this is what you'll be doing when we're dancing together."

He nodded and tried to keep a straight face. If only his siblings could see him now. He'd be teased for sure and for certain.

"You will lead with your left foot. When you move your left foot forward, my right foot will go back, like this." She demonstrated the male step. "This will be you."

Next, she demonstrated her own step backwards. "This is me. Got it?"

He nodded. "I think so. What if I go too fast and I step on your foot?"

Megan lifted a 'your innocence is so adorable' smile. "Come here, let me show you something."

He hopped up and sauntered to where she stood in the middle of his living room.

"Now, get that silly grin off your face. This is serious."

He saluted her and tried not to laugh.

"Elam!" She shook her head and stepped close. No doubt he was testing her patience, but he could tell she did her best not to smile. "Grasp my left hand with your right one and hold it at about shoulder height."

He did as told and she adjusted it accordingly.

"Okay, now put the palm of your left hand on my right shoulder blade." She placed her right hand on his arm. "Okay, great."

"This feels a little awkward." He noticed how close their bodies were and sweat beaded on his forehead.

"Relax, Elam."

He chuckled. "It's hard to with you being this close to me."

"Men." She smiled and shook her head. "Okay, now look down at where your feet are and notice where mine are. Now step forward with your left foot."

He did as told again and she stepped back at the same time.

"See? It's almost like we're on a different track. Since my

leg is on the inside and yours is on the outside, it's impossible for you to step on my foot."

"Now it makes more sense."

"And now you've completed your first step. Let's try it again."

After they'd practiced a few times, he finally felt comfortable. She even played a song from her cell phone and he finally saw how the steps came together with the music. When the lesson was finally over, they both laughed. He didn't know whether it was from relief or because they'd enjoyed being in each other's company. Either way, they both agreed they had fun—in spite of his antics.

He still held her close. "I think I might want to kiss you."

She tucked part of her bottom lip under her teeth and smiled shyly. "You do?" He read the expectation in her mien and she didn't protest, so he took that as permission to do so.

He nodded, his gaze never leaving hers, and leaned down until his lips met hers and their eyes closed. He began tentatively at first, then pulled her closer, his hands entangled with her hair. The kiss deepened and he dropped his hand to her waist drawing her form near until it molded to his. He'd never been this close to any woman, not even Julianna. The feeling was wonderful, but he knew they must stop or they'd soon be doing something they shouldn't. He forced himself to break away.

They were both out of breath, but their mutual attraction won out. He pulled her close once again and continued the kiss, this time pulling her into his lap on the sofa. His lips left hers and he felt her breath hitch as his kiss slowly trailed the delicate skin of her neck then returned to her lips with intensified passion. He desired more. Much more.

"Elam?" Megan said between kisses. "We can't do this."

"I know." He groaned in frustration and forced himself away again.

This time, Megan stood up and combed her fingers through her hair.

Elam stared at her feminine form and his desire for her only increased. His arms ached to pull her close and hold her again. He stepped near.

"I should probably go now." She spoke the words, but stood in place.

Elam frowned, then caressed her face. "I know, but I don't want you to."

She searched his eyes. Did she want the same thing? "You know I can't stay here with you."

He nodded. "*Jah*, you're right. It's late. You should probably go."

"Okay." Her disenchanted gaze met his frown. "You're not upset, are you?"

"Just at myself. I shouldn't have…" He shook his head and sighed.

"Shouldn't have what?"

He eyed her slightly swollen lips. "Kissed you too much. It was unwise."

"I'm sorry."

"You don't have to be sorry. You cannot help being beautiful."

"You think I'm beautiful, Elam?" She sounded surprised, and Elam wondered if nobody had told her before. Wasn't vanity the *Englisch* way?

He nodded. "Very much so."

"Thank you for saying that. I've never really considered myself beautiful. Just okay, I guess."

"No one has told you this?"

"No, never. You're the first." She shook her head. "Not that it matters a whole lot. Beauty is in the eye of the beholder, right?"

Elam raised a brow.

"You've never heard that expression?"

"No."

"It just basically means that each person sees beauty in their own way. What might be the most beautiful thing in the world to one person, could be something someone else thinks is unattractive."

"I see."

She put distance between them by moving to the kitchen and gathering the things she'd brought.

"I'll carry that for you," he offered, relieving her of the slow cooker.

They walked through the door and out to her car. He opened the door for her, and she placed her purse and other items inside.

"You can set that on the floorboard in the back," she suggested.

"Thank you for bringing dinner." He reached over and tucked her hair behind her ear.

She shrugged. "Well, we both had to eat so, why not? Maybe we can do it again sometime."

Elam grinned. "I'd like that."

They stared at each other in silence for probably a full minute, and he wondered what she was thinking. He knew what *he* was thinking—things only a married man should be dwelling on. And he wasn't anywhere near the marrying stage with Megan, so he'd better take a step back before he let things get out of hand.

He leaned forward and briefly kissed her cheek. "Goodnight, Megan."

She slid into her car, closed the door, and turned over the ignition. Elam watched her pull away from the curb, many thoughts swirling in his mind. The main one being what it would be like to be married to Megan.

For the life of him, he just couldn't picture the scenario. Megan was a wonderful girl—she was sweet, beautiful, kind, a great cook. So what was his problem? Was it because she was *Englisch*? That had to be it. He'd never pictured himself married to an *Englisch* girl, not once in all the years he'd been away from the Amish. The only one he'd ever seen himself with was Julianna, but he knew that was now impossible.

He had to give Julie up if he ever hoped to move on, because right now he was stuck at the top of an emotional rollercoaster. At any moment, it could come barreling down.

But he had no clue how to give her up—how to let her go.

NINE

"What do you think of Megan?" Elam turned from the horse he'd been brushing down and pinned his gaze on Zachariah.

Zach's brow rose. "She seems really nice."

"Do you think we make a good match? Could you see us married?"

He pet the mare in front of him and gently placed her harness on. "I don't know, Elam. That's your call to make."

"You don't think so." He frowned.

"No, I didn't say that. It's just, I don't know. Marriage is a lifelong commitment. *Englischers* are so different, you know what I mean? They don't *get* a lot of Amish things because they've never lived it. They tend to be a lot more sensitive about things." Zach stared at him as though contemplating something. "How do you think your folks would react if you took her home to meet them?"

Elam shook his head. "I can't imagine. With her short hair…" He didn't even want to *think* about that conversation.

"*Jah.*" Zach nodded in understanding. "Do you and Megan clash at all?"

"She teaches dancing."

"Dancing? Like ballet?"

"All kinds of dancing."

"And this bothers you?"

Elam shrugged, recalling the last time they'd danced together. "Not really. It's just...different."

"So, has she taught *you* to dance?"

"Mm...do I have to answer that?"

Zach pointed at him. "Yes, you do."

"We've danced a time or two."

Zach grinned. "And?"

"And it feels...sensual. You know, her body close to mine. It's tempting."

Zach stuck his right foot into the stirrup and hoisted himself onto the horse. Elam noticed that over the years, his cousin had adapted more and more to the use of his prosthetic leg. So much so, that Elam sometimes forgot he even had it. But it was times like this that he noticed and sent up an extra prayer for his cousin. It was one thing to watch someone with a disability, but it was an entirely different thing to *be* the one with the disability. For someone who was whole, he couldn't imagine walking in Zach's shoes even for one day.

Zach pulled him from his musing. "I could see where that could cause problems. Does she dance this way with others too?"

He shook his head and mounted his horse as well. "She teaches couples, who dance with each other."

"Elam, are you telling me this because you're attracted to her? Because you want to *be* with her?" Zach frowned.

"*Ach*, I've definitely thought of it. But we wouldn't unless we were married." Elam shrugged. "It's just making me think a lot more about marriage."

"Marriage is about a lot more than just the physical part. You haven't even known Megan long enough to be considering marriage, in my opinion. It's too soon, Elam."

"I realize that. I'm not planning to propose to her tomorrow or anything, okay?" He tried keeping the frustration out of his voice. "I'm sorry."

Zach nodded, then wisely changed the subject. "Have you gone back home recently?"

"No." Elam shook his head. "After I found out about Julie…it was too much."

"How did she die? You never told me." Zach made a clicking sound to encourage his horse to trot a little faster.

"I'm not exactly sure."

"I find it odd that no one told you about her death sooner. Don't you?"

"It's not like I've really been in contact with anyone. And we don't talk about too much when I'm with my folks."

"I know, but you know how the Amish grapevine is. You think someone would have gotten word to you. She *was* your *aldi* at one time. If for nothing else, to get you to go back home."

Elam shrugged and sighed. "Why are we talking about this again?"

"Have you fully made peace with your past, Elam? Because if you're serious about moving on with Megan, I think it's essential."

"I do have a lot of unanswered questions, but I don't know if I'll ever find those answers."

"I think you should try. You need full closure before you can truly move forward. That's my two cents, I'll send you my bill." Zach laughed, lightening the moment.

Zach was right, Elam realized. He did need those answers. But the question was, how did he go about getting them?

As difficult as it was, Elam turned into the lane of his folks' property. He loathed the fact that his parents were required to have limited contact with him due to his shunning. It was just one item on his list of things he wished he could change about the Amish culture.

He knew there were some Amish districts where family was allowed to have full contact with their loved ones, Amish or no, but theirs was not one of them. For this reason, he'd mostly stayed away from his family. He understood that they chose to live this way, and he respected that they didn't wish to be at odds with the leaders, lest they themselves be put in the *Bann* as well.

He knew his family loved him, and he loved them, but he didn't love the manmade rules they'd been forced to live under. Many times, he'd felt like it was an emotional manipulation tactic used to control those in the church, but he was at a loss as to what to do about it.

He'd only been back a handful of times because of this, and he'd questioned many times whether he had done the right thing in leaving. However, staying Amish would have meant keeping his faith in Christ to himself and that was something that went against the Scriptural mandate of going into all the world to preach the Gospel. *We ought to obey God rather than men.* So, essentially, he could have remained Amish and been shunned for speaking the truth in love, or he could leave the bonds of the church and worship God in freedom.

But what about his family? What about his Amish friends? They needed the truth as much as he had. How could he not share this with them?

Like Julianna. That was something he was sure he'd regret for as long as he lived, perhaps for all eternity.

It wasn't that he hadn't shared Jesus with his family. He had. But each time he brought up the subject he'd been shut down. They'd been taught that to be 'saved' was an *Englisch* doctrine. But he now knew that wasn't true. As a matter of fact, it came directly from the Bible.

Any time he thought of the voluminous verses on the subject, it baffled him that the Amish ministers chose to ignore them. *For whosoever shall call upon the name of the Lord shall be saved. For by grace ye are saved, through faith, and that not of yourselves, it is the gift of God, not of works lest any man should boast. For there is none other name under heaven given among men whereby we must be saved.*

What further baffled him was how they equated that to believe those verses, one must be engulfed in the sin of pride. If anything, the opposite was true. The Bible clearly stated that salvation was a *gift* of God. How, then, could it possibly be prideful? And weren't we encouraged to boast in the Lord? It seemed to him that what *would* be boastful was to think that your Amish group was better than the others because of your buggy style or your style of dress or one of the many other things his former community believed brought them closer to God or made them less worldly.

With these thoughts, he sighed and stepped out of his vehicle. Today, no matter how painful it might be, he was here to find answers about Julianna.

Elam now sat on the porch of his folks' place, sipping the iced tea his mother had placed on the table beside him. It irked him that they still weren't allowed to invite him inside the house, but he would take what he could get. At least they still talked to him.

"Someone continues to send us money in the mail every month." One side of his father's mouth lifted. "It wonders me who keeps sending it."

"Must be from *Der Herr, jah?*" Elam figured his parents knew the money was sent from him, but he wouldn't acknowledge it. If he did, his folks would probably be required to send it back to him. So he chose to stay anonymous. "How are you and *Mamm* getting by?"

"As *gut* as can be expected, I reckon. And you?" His father had never been one to complain.

"I'm doing well." Elam smiled.

"Do you have an *aldi?*"

His gaze moved to his younger sister, pondering her question. She'd grown up so much since he'd left. Just barely a teen when her brother had jumped the fence, now she was no doubt attending singings and possibly being courted by a young Amish man. Her eyes sparkled with the expectancy of youth.

Elam smiled. "I do. Her name is Megan. She goes to my church."

"Will you marry her?"

He loved the straightforwardness of his Amish culture. If something needed to be said, it was. No worrying about offending another person because they didn't get offended easily. Not like some of the *Englisch* with whom he had to watch his p's and q's. That was one reason he enjoyed spending time with his cousin Zach.

His brow shot up. "I might, but not too soon. We haven't even been dating that long."

"What's she like?"

He shrugged. "She's really nice. Y'all would like her. She likes to dance and cook."

His sister's eyes went large. "Do *you* dance?"

"I do." He nodded. "Although I'm not very good at it. But Megan's great."

"That's sinful." His mother frowned. "You shouldn't be talking of such things with your sister here."

"*Mamm*, two people aren't any closer when they're dancing than they are when courting." He reminded his mother of their Amish courting customs, which included a quiet evening alone with your significant other, many times with a young woman sitting on the young man's lap. The *Englisch* didn't have a corner on temptation. No, it dwelt in every culture—in every heart.

"How is work?" His father asked, obviously wanting to change the subject.

"Work's great. I'm staying busy."

"I see you bought yourself a truck."

"I did. Do you like it? I could take you for a ride."

"You know that is not our way." His father frowned, but Elam knew that he would love to if it didn't carry any negative consequences.

Elam sighed, then a sly grin creeped up his mouth. "You could always duck when we pass by any Amish." He chuckled.

To his surprise, his father did too. "It is tempting."

"Henry!" his mother chided.

"He was joking, *Mamm*."

"You shouldn't joke about such things. We don't need any more trouble with the leaders."

Elam's brow shot up and his eyes moved to his father. "*More* trouble? Has Bishop Hershberger been giving you grief? What for?"

"*Nee*, Elam. It is not your concern." His father frowned at his mother. Apparently, they weren't willing to share this with him.

"They're thinking Danny will follow in your footsteps." His sister volunteered, much to their parents' chagrin.

"Where is he?" He knew the pressure families faced when one of their own jumped the fence, and he regretted that his actions probably caused them much sorrow. But he never dreamed his brother would become *Englisch* too.

"Out with his friends."

That figured. That was where he would have been at his brother's age.

He tried to find a way to turn the conversation around. "How's everyone else doing?"

"Same, pretty much. Everyone's just living their lives. Lots of babies born lately. Marlin's John's Rachel and Jerry's Clara both had girls. Then Fancy Jake's Fannie had twins, two boys." His mother seemed happy to share that bit of information with him.

"How's Julianna Yoder's family?"

"Doing fine, far as I know. Saw Elnora at a quilting last week." His mother nodded.

"Can you tell me about Julianna? How did she pass away?"

Did he notice a peculiar look pass between his father and mother? "That story is not ours to tell. You'll need to talk to her family."

That wasn't likely to happen any time soon. The wounds of humiliation had cut deep and approaching her father after he'd flat out cut him off from his daughter was not something he was willing to do in this lifetime. For this reason, he decided to give up on his quest to find answers about Julianna's death.

Just knowing she was gone was enough emotional turmoil to deal with.

TEN

Elam pulled the truck into his driveway and immediately noticed someone near his front door. From where he sat, the person appeared to be a stranger. He stepped out of the pickup and hesitantly walked toward his front door.

"May I help you?"

The stranger spun around. "Elam?" A huge grin spread across his face. "It's me, Danny. Your brother."

Elam stepped forward and engulfed his younger brother in a bear hug.

"You're so big." The comment was an understatement, seeing his young brother towered over him by about six inches. "Sheesh! How tall are you?"

He shrugged. "Six-four, I think."

"Man, I don't know if I would have recognized you, had you not said anything. What have you been eating, anyway?" Elam laughed.

"Just *Mamm's* cooking."

"What are you doing here? How'd you find me?"

"I used the internet at the library."

"I see." Elam unlocked the door and turned the handle. Normally, he would have entered through the side door that led through the garage. "Want to come inside?"

"Thought you'd never ask." Danny followed him inside. "This looks like a decent place."

Elam chuckled. "Thanks. I think."

"How many rooms does it have?"

"It's a two-bedroom, one-bath. Just over a thousand square feet."

"It's tiny compared to *Daed's* place."

Elam shrugged. "Well, it's just me. I don't need much."

"Any land?"

"Just a small backyard." He moved to the back door. "Which reminds me." He opened the door and found Scramble wagging his tale.

"Is that your dog?"

"Yep. Danny, this is Scramble. Scramble meet Danny."

His brother crouched down and offered Scramble a handshake. "Shake, buddy?"

The dog lifted his paw.

"Good boy."

Scramble whined and cocked his head at Elam.

"I'll get your food in just a minute, Scram." He opened up a large trash can he kept on the back patio and scooped up some dog food and placed it in Scramble's dish. "You're going to have to wait for your walk, though."

Elam closed the door and turned to Danny. "Would you like a drink?"

Danny's brow shot up. "Beer?"

"No. Not in *this* house. Tea, soda, or water?"

Danny sighed. "Soda, it is. Got root beer?"

"*That* kind of beer, I do have." He chuckled. "Why don't you take a seat?"

Danny plopped down onto the couch, a futon that he sometimes used for snoozing when he returned home from work dog tired.

Elam handed his brother a bottle of root beer and swallowed a drink of his own. "So, what have you been up to, little brother?"

"Working. Getting into trouble."

"That's not good. The trouble part. Working *is* good. Where are you working at?"

"The Stolzfoos Ranch."

Elam frowned at the mention of his former rival's surname. "Really? They pay you well?"

Danny shrugged. "Fair enough, I guess. Anyway, that's where I found the trouble too."

"Oh, no. What did you do?"

"I started courting Tabitha Stolzfoos." Danny grimaced. "We think she might be in the family way."

"Oh, no. You didn't..." Elam sighed. "*Jah*, I'd say that's pretty big trouble. What are you going to do about it? Do

Mamm and *Daed* know?"

Danny shook his head. "We're not even sure yet. But we're thinking of leaving the Amish."

"Why?"

"*You're* asking me why? I thought of all people, you would understand."

"I do. But *if* Tabitha is pregnant, you're going to need the support of the Amish community. You don't want to have a *boppli* out in the *Englisch* world. It's hard enough just making it as a single man with no family support. But having a family and doing it? I don't think it's a wise idea."

"I don't know how much support we'd get."

"I doubt Tabitha's family is going to abandon her." He thought about Tabitha Stolzfoos. She couldn't be more than sixteen or seventeen.

"We're scared to tell our folks. Neither one of us is baptized yet."

"And rightfully so. Confessing our sins is never easy. But it's the right thing to do."

Danny took a deep breath and nodded. "You're probably right."

Elam clasped his brother's shoulder. "I have confidence in you. You can do this. A man will admit to his mistakes, learn from them, and move on."

"Thanks, Elam. I knew you would help me make sense of things."

Elam couldn't fathom being in his brother's predicament—

not even eighteen yet and possibly becoming a father? Deep regret settled in his heart, just knowing the turmoil it would bring his folks. "I'm glad you confided in me. Keep me updated, will ya?"

"*Jah.*"

Elam eyed his empty bottle. "If you're done with your root beer, I'll challenge you to a game of basketball. There's a school across the street, and Scramble would welcome a walk."

Danny handed him his bottle and grinned. "You're on. But first, I want to see what's in your garage."

He found his brother's request amusing. "My garage?" Did his brother want to work out on his home gym?

"I've heard rumors."

"Rumors? What kind of rumors?"

"Oh, ones involving two wheels and a lot of speed."

Elam laughed. "So, you want to see my motorcycle?"

"See it, drool over it, ride it." Danny smiled.

"You know how to ride?"

"I'm a fast learner."

ELEVEN

"It's important to guard your heart against temptation." Mike's words were timely.

Elam briefly glanced in Megan's direction and nodded in agreement with the leader's statement. He thought of the last time they'd been together, dancing. It had taken a lot of self- control not to do the things he'd wanted to.

"What do you think, Elam?"

Elam's eyes widened. *Oh, shoot, what were they talking about? Temptation?* "About?"

"Bowling in a few of weeks." Chase raised a brow.

"Oh, yeah, that sounds great." He forced a smile.

Chase laughed. "It sounds like someone was off in la la land. That seems to happen a lot lately."

Megan headed toward them and his eyes locked with hers. "Mm-hm."

"Ah, I see." Chase chuckled and it broke Elam's concentration. His friend patted him on the back. "Go get her, buddy."

"Yeah." Was all Elam could come up with.

"Hi, guys." Megan's smile could light up the whole room, it seemed. "You ready, Elam?"

He nodded. "Let's go."

"Hey, I'll see you two at church tomorrow." Chase's voice echoed behind them as they neared the door.

"Yep, see ya." Elam stepped out with his girl at his side. He turned to her. "Did we have plans for tonight?"

Her face brightened once again. "Movies at your house, remember?"

"That's right. I've already got the popcorn and ingredients for root beer floats."

"Root beer floats?"

"You do like them, don't you?"

"Like them, yes. The question is, *should* I like them?" She patted her flat belly.

"Once in a while won't hurt, *jah*?"

"*Jah*?" she teased. "I love it when your Amish slips out every now and then. It's cute."

"Cute?" He laughed.

"It's endearing."

He pushed the button on his key fob to unlock the truck door, then pulled open her door for her and helped her up into his truck. He was tempted to kiss her then and there. "Did you bring the movies you mentioned?"

"Yep, they're right here in my purse." She held the movies up. "Firefighters or cops?"

He slid into the driver's seat. "Both sound good. Probably cops, though. I used to want to be one."

"A cop? How come this is the first time I'm hearing about this?"

He shrugged and turned the key in the ignition. "Never came up, I guess."

"Is that what got you involved in helping out at the youth center?"

He smiled, turning out of the church parking lot. "Yes, actually. I enjoy spending time with the boys there. A lot of them come from broken homes without a father. Since I am shunned, I feel like I can relate to them in a way."

"It's important for them to have positive male role models, I think. What do you do when you're there?"

"Pretty much just play basketball, or whatever else is going on. They have all sorts of activities and games and such. It's a great chance to get to know them. Once in a while, we'll just go for a walk or a bike ride on the outdoor trail they have on the property, and we'll talk."

"I bet they enjoy spending time with you."

Elam nodded and tapped his fingers on the steering wheel, while waiting for the traffic light to change. "I like to spend time with them too. It's kind of like having younger brothers. And since I don't get to spend much time with my actual brothers, I think it meets a need for me too."

"Do you share your experiences of your past Amish life?"

"Sometimes."

"How do they react to that?"

"Well, most of them can't fathom having a large intact family that shares meals and works together. It's like a dream to them."

"Yet, you left all that. Do they find that crazy?"

"Somewhat, but I think they understand. There's more to it than what folks see on the outside. It's a very restrictive lifestyle." He pulled the car up to his driveway and killed the engine.

"I can imagine." Megan turned to him. "I'd love to go on a buggy ride someday."

Elam chuckled. "You would?"

She nodded.

He exited the truck, opened her door for her, and helped her down. The truck seemed even bigger when Megan was near it. "I think I might be able to arrange something like that."

"Really?" Her eyes lit up and he felt like kissing her as she stood just in front of him.

He leaned forward and placed both of his hands on the body of the truck, pinning her petite frame between himself and the vehicle. "Would you like that?" His low voice sounded almost like a whisper to him and he knew she understood his double entendre.

At her silent nod, he leaned down and met her soft lips. The kiss was slow and gentle and sweet. He lingered there an extra minute, enjoying each delicate movement.

"Mm…that was *really* nice." It almost felt as though he were entranced, gazing into her warm caramel eyes. The appearing of stars in the sky enhanced the mood even more. What would it be like to spend the night with her in his arms? He lightly caressed her cheek, debating whether kissing her again would be a good idea.

A car whizzed by and it broke the moment. Suddenly, he was aware of their location—still standing in his driveway. The public display of affection felt very non-Amish.

"We should go inside," Megan suggested. He didn't miss the subtle blushing of her cheeks, even in the darkening night.

He cleared his throat. "Good idea. We have popcorn to make."

Moments later the aroma of popcorn filled the air. Elam poured the melted butter over the top of the bowl and mixed it in well, in an attempt to cover each kernel.

"Do you want salt on it," he called to Megan, who was in the living room preparing the movie.

"Just a little, please. If it's too salty I won't be able to eat it."

"Should I make the floats now or later?"

"Now. Sweet and salty go well together." She peered around the corner. "Need help?"

"Nah, I think I got it." He eyed her clothing. "You changed."

She glanced down at her sweat pants and V-neck t-shirt.

"You don't mind, do you? I like to be comfy when I watch movies."

He stepped near and pulled her close. "I don't mind at all. You look cute in everything." He briefly kissed her, then turned back to the task at hand.

Megan pulled glassware from his cupboard and set it on the counter. Elam placed a couple of scoops of vanilla ice cream in each glass and then poured in the soda.

"Okay. I think we're ready. Did you figure out my DVD player?" He handed Megan her drink and the bowl of popcorn. "I'll grab some paper towels."

"Yep. It's all ready to go." She frowned in the direction of his futon.

"I'm sorry my couch isn't more comfortable."

"Oh, no. It's fine. I was just thinking it would be nice if we had some pillows."

"I have a couple on my bed. You can use my extra one."

"That sounds perfect. Do you have a throw too?"

"A throw?"

"You know, like a small blanket that you throw over the couch?"

"Okay, I'll see what I can find." He rushed to his room, excitement of spending the evening with his girl growing with each second. He returned with the two pillows and his fleece camo blanket.

"That'll do." She grinned.

"Get up a sec. This futon reclines. It'll be more

comfortable for watching movies." He quickly adjusted the couch, handed Megan her pillow and blanket, and sank down next to her. He leaned over and nuzzled her cheek.

"Now, you're going to have to watch this because I don't want you to miss anything. Okay?" Megan pushed the play button on the remote control. "It's a good movie."

He forced himself away from her and fixed his eyes on the screen the moment it started. This was going to be a fun night.

TWELVE

Elam pried his eyes open. Megan lay nestled in his arms, a pillow between them and his camo blanket tucked under her arms. The second movie they'd watched, the one about the firefighters, had been interesting but it appeared they had both fallen asleep. The television was still on, seemingly frozen on the home screen of the feature film.

What time was it, anyway? He looked toward one of the windows where the curtain was drawn. Was it light outside already? *Oh, no.*

"Meg, wake up." He kissed the top of her head and lightly rubbed her arms, not wanting to startle her from sleep. She sighed deeply, as though lost in a dream.

"Megan, babe." This time he leaned over enough to kiss her lips. He knew she'd awakened when she responded. He smiled.

"Elam?" She touched his face, but her eyes stayed closed.

"It's morning, Megan. We need to get up."

She bolted upright, knocking his chin in the process.

"Ow." He rubbed his chin, now stubbled with the facial hair that had grown overnight.

"Sorry." She leaned over and pecked his cheek, then frowned. "Did you say morning? What time is it?" She shot up from the couch.

"I don't know. I haven't looked yet."

"Where did I put my phone?" She looked around.

"Is it in the kitchen? I think that's where you left your purse."

She hurried to the kitchen and pulled out her cell phone. "Oh, shoot. It's nine o'clock, Elam! Church is in thirty minutes. And my dad tried to call."

Just then, the doorbell rang.

"Oh, no. It's my dad! I know it is." Sheer panic set on her face. She looked down at her sweats and t-shirt. "I need to change. I have to get ready for church."

"It's okay, Megan. I'll answer the door." His voice sounded a lot calmer than his nerves felt.

Before he could even walk to the door, she bolted for the bathroom.

Elam took a deep breath and looked through the peephole. Megan had been correct. Sure enough, her father stood on the other side of the door. He reluctantly pulled it open.

"Good morning, sir." Elam nodded.

"Hello, Elam. I hope I didn't wake you up." Megan's father stared at something above Elam's head. Must've been his hair. Was it sticking up?

Elam frowned. He hadn't even thought to look in the mirror or comb his hair. "No, sir. You didn't awaken me."

"Okay, good. The reason I'm here is because I haven't been able to get ahold of Megan and I was wondering if you've possibly seen her. I tried calling her cell last night and this morning. Nothing. We drove by her house and her car is still there, but when I knocked on her door she didn't answer. I'm terribly worried."

"She's here," Elam admitted.

"Here?" His brow furrowed.

Elam stepped aside and gestured for the deacon to enter his home.

"Just a minute." Elam left Megan's father at the door. He walked down the hall to the bathroom and lightly knocked on the door. "Megan? Your father is here."

She opened the door and shared a terrified look with him.

Elam leaned close and whispered. "He's by the front door."

She whispered back, "Does he look angry?"

Elam shrugged.

Megan walked in the direction of where her father stood. "Dad? What are you doing here?"

"No, what are *you* doing here? I've tried to call you since last night. We went by your house this morning. Where have you been?"

"Sorry. I had my cell phone on silent."

"You didn't answer my question. Where have you been all this time?" He repeated, his neck and face darkening to a maroon color. "Don't tell me you spent the night with Elam."

"I was here."

"The whole time?" He glowered in Elam's direction, and Elam wished he could disappear into the wall.

Megan's hands shook. "Yes. But it's not what you think it is. We just watched some movies and we fell asleep."

"And you expect everybody to believe that?" His hand practically screeched through his hair.

"No. I don't care what everyone believes. But I expect *you* to believe it!" The tears in Megan's eyes made Elam want to wrap his arms around her. But somehow he didn't think that would help the situation at the moment.

Megan's father sighed. "Megan, I've been worried about you. Everyone's been worried about you. I tried to call. Mom and I went by last night. And then when you still didn't answer your door or your phone this morning, we nearly called the police. We tried everyone we could think of. Pastor, Mike, everyone. The last person we talked to said you'd left the singles class in Elam's truck. I never dreamed you'd stay here with him. All. Night. Long." He frowned. "That's not in your character."

"Dad. I already told you the truth. We watched movies and we fell asleep. It was an innocent mistake."

"Innocent?" His gaze bounced from Elam to Megan and they both nodded in confirmation. He took a deep breath. "Okay. Let's just forget all this happened and make sure it doesn't happen again. Do I make myself clear?"

Elam swallowed. "Yes, sir"

"Yes, Dad."

"I think you should ride to church with us today, rather than with Elam. It will look better that way." Her father insisted.

"I'll probably be late. I have to shower and get ready," Elam grimaced.

Megan lifted a wobbly smile. "Okay." When she threw her arms around him, he didn't resist, although it felt awkward with her father there.

"I'll see you later?" He whispered in her ear.

She nodded, then followed her father out the door.

Elam watched and sighed as they drove away. That had to be one of the most uncomfortable situations he'd ever been in. Church this morning would probably be even worse. Would there be rumors flying around that he and the deacon's daughter had spent the night together? He was tempted to skip church altogether. He pondered it for a moment, then his words to his brother came back to haunt him. *A man will admit to his mistakes, learn from them, and move on.*

He exhaled loudly. Time to put his own advice into practice.

THIRTEEN

"Hey, thanks for letting me ride your bike. That was a blast." Danny beamed. "I told you it would be nothing for me to learn."

"You did well for your first time. But you should really watch your speed, especially since you won't wear my helmet."

"When did you become such a worry wart?"

Elam frowned. "I have a right to be concerned about my baby brother. And *my* motorcycle."

About a block from the house, Elam smiled and his pace quickened. Megan had pulled up to the house in her adorable little car. "She's here."

The curiosity dancing in his brother's eyes didn't escape his notice. "Is that your girl?"

Elam nodded.

Danny released a low whistle. "Impressive, brother. She's cute."

Elam had often thought the same thing. As a matter of

fact, 'cute' was the perfect word to describe Megan. "Shh…" he warned, as Megan approached.

"Hi." Megan's eyes sparkled.

"Hi." Elam lightly bumped her hip with his and winked. "Meg, this is my baby brother, Danny."

"Younger brother," Danny corrected, glaring at Elam.

Megan laughed. "Nice to meet you, Danny."

Elam eyed the dish in her hands. "What ya got there?"

"Dinner. But it still needs to go in the oven." She grinned. "Danny's welcome to join us."

Elam lifted his brow toward his brother.

"It's tempting, but I'm sure you two would like to be alone," Danny said.

"You sure? It's no problem. Megan and I will still get our alone time." He glanced at Megan, who nodded in agreement. "Why don't you stay a little bit?"

"*Ach*, I better not. I'm supposed to pick up Tabitha tonight. As a matter of fact, may I use your phone to call a driver?" Danny chuckled. "Unless I can take your bike?"

"Won't that get you into trouble?" Elam's brow raised.

Danny shook his head and a sly grin crept across his face. "No more than what I'm already in. And *you're* already in the *Bann*, so…What do you say?"

Megan looked back and forth at each of them, seemingly enjoying their banter.

Elam sighed. "Why do I have a feeling I'm going to regret

this?" He pointed to his brother. "No driving too fast, and I want you to wear the helmet."

"Seriously? You'll let me take it?" His brother's excitement reminded him of the first time he rode on a motorcycle.

"When can you have it back to me?"

"Friday?"

Elam grimaced. He didn't know if allowing his brother to have his motorcycle that long was the wisest idea. "Okay. But no giving rides."

"You're kidding. Not even Tabitha?"

"*Especially* not Tabitha."

"Aw, man."

Elam shrugged and handed him his phone. "Fine, then call your driver."

Danny pushed the phone back to him. "Okay, no rides."

"Promise me."

"I promise." Danny shook his head and looked at Megan. "Is he always like this?"

She shared a gaze with Elam. "Caring? Yes."

"I better get going before this mother hen lays down any more rules." Danny looked at Elam. "Key?"

He reached into his pocket. "Have a care now."

"Yeah, yeah." He snatched the keys from Elam's hand and jogged into the garage. "See ya Friday."

"You better." He watched as his brother removed his hat and put the helmet on his head.

"What am I going to do with this thing?" Danny held up his Amish hat.

"Do you have an extra one at home?"

"Not a good one."

"Turn around."

Danny did as told. Elam took his hat and placed it under the suspenders on his back.

"Will that hold?"

Elam shrugged. "It should."

Megan chimed in. "Do you have a backpack?"

Elam leaned over and kissed her. "*That* is a great idea. Hold on a second, brother."

A few minutes later, Elam and Megan watched as Danny pulled out of the driveway and headed down the road on Elam's motorcycle.

Elam sent up a brief prayer. *Please don't let me live to regret this.*

FOURTEEN

Elam pulled a nail from his toolbelt and hammered it into the structure that would eventually become a playhouse for some lucky little girl. The customer had insisted the mini cottage be painted pink with white trim and a porch that wrapped all the way around.

Elam laughed to himself. The lengths *Englischers* went to just to make their *kinner* happy. He thought about his own sisters and the things they will have accomplished by the time they step into womanhood. They'd be capable of running an entire household before they reached their mid-teens.

His cell phone vibrated in his pocket, distracting him from his musings.

"Hello?" he answered, expecting Megan or Zach to be on the other line.

A timid voice answered back. "*Hallo*, is this Elam?"

He had no doubt it was an Amish woman. "Yes, this is Elam speaking." He answered in their native tongue. "Who is this?"

"It's Tabitha Stolzfoos. Your brother has been in an accident."

His heart pounded. "Danny? Is he okay?"

"He's in the hospital. He said to call you."

Oh, good. He sighed in relief. If Danny was able to tell Tabitha to call, that meant he wasn't dead. "Please, Tabitha. Tell me where."

After giving Elam the needed hospital information, they hung up. Elam sighed. No doubt, Danny had been on his motorcycle. No doubt, the leaders would use this as a lesson to warn others to avoid worldly possessions. No doubt, *he'd* be blamed for loaning it to his brother.

He couldn't dwell on that now. He had to go check on Danny and assure himself that his brother was okay. Because if he wasn't, Elam didn't know how he was going to live with himself.

He bowed his head. *Thank you, Gott, for protecting Danny. Please don't let him be injured too badly. And help him to recover quickly.*

As soon as Elam entered the hospital, he located the nearest information desk to inquire of his brother's whereabouts. The attendant hadn't said he was in ICU, so that was a good sign. He now walked with purpose in his step, searching for the room number they'd given him.

Remarkably, the waiting room had been empty when he passed by. He'd expected it to contain at least a few Amish well-wishers, given his brother's circumstances. He'd hoped he could reach his brother before anyone else in the community. Maybe he'd get his wish. He wanted to hear straight from Danny what had happened.

He cautiously opened the door to his brother's hospital room, not exactly sure what he'd find. The curtain had been pulled and the bed nearest to the door sat empty.

He would have moved forward, but he didn't want to interrupt the conversation taking place on the other side of the curtain. He strained to hear the voices, attempting to make out who was visiting.

"See, Tabitha. This is what becomes of someone who doesn't follow the old ways. Before you know it, he'll jump the fence just like his brother." Elam had no doubt it was Tabitha's father spewing the words of warning. "I forbid you to keep seeing him."

"No!" A young woman—who he assumed to be Tabitha—cried. "I won't."

Elam's eyes widened. He had never heard an Amish woman speak that way to one in authority. His sister wouldn't dare address their father in such a manner. Surely, Danny would have his hands full if he were to marry Tabitha Stolzfoos.

"You will do as I say," her father retorted.

"But, *Dat*. I'm in the family way! I'm going to have Danny's baby."

Elam grimaced. That probably wasn't the best way to announce the future arrival of their *kinskinner*. He regretted being there and contemplated leaving the room. He would if he thought he could escape unnoticed. Should he interrupt?

He heard a gasp, most likely Tabitha's mother—or maybe his own?

"Is this true?" Tabitha's father asked. Who, Elam didn't know.

Danny responded. "*Jah.*"

"I should have known something like this would happen. That's what I get for hiring a Zook," her father fumed. "You're fired, Daniel."

"But you can't fire him!" Tabitha cried.

"I just did. Now come, Tabitha. You're going home with your *mudder* and me."

Elam blew out a breath. This was a really awkward place to be at the moment. He couldn't stay hidden any longer.

He took a few steps and moved the curtain. "Danny!" he said, ignoring the grunt exuded by Tabitha's father.

Elam feigned ignorance and looked at each of them. "I hope I didn't interrupt."

"No. We were just leaving." Tabitha's father glowered at Elam, then at Danny. "We'll discuss this situation later— before the leaders," he threatened.

"Goodbye, Danny." Tabitha's longing gaze met his brother's before she was whisked out of the room by her folks.

Elam was thankful for the time alone with Danny. He examined his brother's condition. Other than his arm being in a sling, a bandage on his head, and a few scrapes on his face, he looked all right.

"Are you okay? What happened?" Elam frowned.

"I'll replace your bike."

"We can discuss that later. It doesn't matter right now. I want to know what happened."

"I was going around the curve. I don't know what happened for sure. Maybe we didn't—"

"*We?*" Elam's brow shot up. "You had someone on the bike with you?" He'd *promised* he wouldn't. Elam couldn't stop the disappointment from displaying on his face.

Danny nodded. "Marlin Wickey."

His fists tightened, causing his fingernails to dig into his palms. "Is he injured?"

"I don't know. I haven't heard. They brought us in separate ambulances. I asked the nurse, but she wouldn't say."

Elam rubbed his forehead. "Have *Mamm* and *Daed* been here?"

"*Nee.* But they probably will be any time." Danny shook his head. "I can't believe Tabitha's father won't let her see me no more."

Elam locked eyes with his brother. "If she's carrying your *boppli*, you can be assured you'll see her. Her father is probably just upset right now. And understandably so."

"I want to marry her. But how can I, now that I don't have a job?"

"You'll find work. Zooks always find a way to get what they want."

Danny smiled, a hint of mischief gleaming in his eye. "*Jah*, you're right."

Just then, the hospital room door opened and a couple of Amish men from the community walked in.

Elam lightly clasped his brother's shoulder. "I'll leave you to your visitors. Call me later, okay?"

Danny agreed.

"I'm glad you're still alive."

"*Jah*, me too."

FIFTEEN

Clam stared at the empty space in his garage where his motorcycle used to be just a week ago, reminiscing about the fun times he'd had riding it. Chances were, he wouldn't be getting it back. Ever.

He was quite certain his insurance wouldn't pay to replace it, since his brother had been unlicensed. And he wasn't about to make Danny pay him back if he had a family on the way. If only he'd said no to his brother's request to use his bike. It would be a decision he'd most likely always regret.

At least he still had his truck. He'd thought a motorcycle and a truck had been the perfect combination. One could be used for hauling things and traveling during the colder months, and the other could be used for quick or economical trips to wherever when the weather was nice.

He stopped his musing and remembered his reason for entering the garage in the first place. Today was the day he'd meet up with the guys at the YMCA. It was something he'd been doing twice a month since learning about the youth mentoring program. They'd be bummed to hear his motorcycle riding days were over. He'd wanted to loan the bike to some of the guys in the past when they'd expressed their desire to take a ride, but it had been discouraged. Something about liability issues, they'd said.

He pushed the button to open the garage door and practically jumped out of his skin when he saw his brother standing there.

"They let you out already?" Elam teased, but his brother's expression did not match his own. Were there tears in his eyes? "Danny, what's wrong?"

"Marlin didn't make it."

"What? He...he died?" Elam stared at his brother in disbelief. "Oh, no."

"I don't know what to do." Danny shrugged, no doubt gripped with the same feelings Elam was now having. Regret, helplessness, guilt.

"I'm sorry, Danny." Elam frowned.

He shrugged again, and Elam got the feeling his brother was most likely walking around in a state of shock. He'd felt the same way when he'd learned of Julianna's death. It was still difficult to believe it was true. Even now.

"I feel like I don't know what to do now. He was baptized, Elam. I'm sure I sent him straight to Hell."

Elam's eyes flew wide. "No, Danny. That's not true. Riding a motorcycle doesn't send a person to Hell, even if they are baptized."

"But he was disobeying the *Ordnung*."

"Come on, Danny. Come inside. Let's have some root beer and a snack." Elam led his brother into the house, grabbed a bottle of soda from the fridge, and thrust it toward his brother. "There's a bag of chips in that cupboard right there. Go ahead and take them out. I need to make a quick phone call."

After calling the supervisor of the youth program and informing him of his circumstances, Elam grabbed his Bible and joined his brother at the table.

"Is your girl coming over today?" Danny asked.

"No, I usually have other plans on Saturday afternoon. But I cancelled them to spend time with you." He regretted missing out on time with the guys, but family came first. Fortunately, the singles class had been cancelled tonight and Megan had plans with her family.

"What is that? An *Englisch* Bible?"

"*Jah*. It's the same as our German one, just in *Englisch*." Elam flipped the Bible open. "I want to show you something, Danny."

His brother eyed him warily.

Elam held up his hand. "Just bear with me a minute, okay?"

Danny nodded.

"You said that you think Marlin is in Hell, right?"

"*Jah*."

"Danny, what do you think it takes for a person to go to Heaven?"

His brother shrugged. "Obeying your parents, the church, the *Ordnung*. I don't know. Lots of things, I reckon."

Elam shook his head. "That's where you're wrong. Look here at what this says is required for Heaven." He pointed to the verse and read it aloud. *"He that believeth on the Son—*this is talking about Jesus Christ, the Son of God—*hath everlasting life: and he that believeth not the Son shall not see life; but the wrath of God abideth on him."* He turned to another place. "And here, the Bible says, *That if thou shalt confess with thy mouth the Lord Jesus, and shalt believe in thine heart that God hath raised him from the dead, thou shalt be saved.* So, here, the Bible shows us that belief in Jesus is what it takes to be saved. But belief is not just *knowing*, not a head knowledge, but a *heart* knowledge."

Danny frowned. "I'm not sure I know what that means."

"Do you love Tabitha?"

Danny smiled, but his eyes took on a far away, sad look. "Yes, very much."

"How do you know you love her?"

He shrugged. "Well, I think about her a lot—probably too much. I want to be with her all the time. I would do anything for her."

"See, those things show that you love her. It's something on the inside that comes out on the outside—it is a heart knowledge. If you were to say that you love Tabitha, but showed no evidence of it, I would question your love. *She* would question your love."

"How does this relate to believing in Jesus—with your heart?"

"Well, if you have a heart knowledge—faith in Christ—then, yes it *should* show in what you say, do, and how you act. But those things are *not* what places that knowledge in your heart—that knowledge comes from God. He calls and you respond to His calling by faith. Understand?"

"I think so." He nodded. "So, if that's all it takes to go to Heaven, then why don't the leaders teach that?"

"That's a very good question, Danny." Elam rubbed is chin. "My guess is either they don't know this truth themselves, or they want to keep the Amish traditions alive and so they just keep on teaching the same thing that was taught to them—that you have to keep the *Ordnung*."

"But if keeping the *Ordnung* and being Amish doesn't get us to Heaven, then what's the point?"

"God sees things differently than man does. He doesn't look at what's on the outside, He looks straight through to your heart. You can be Amish and go to Heaven, if you believe in Jesus. You can be *Englisch* and go to Heaven, if you believe in Jesus. On the other hand, you can be Amish and go to Hell, if you have a heart of unbelief. Or you can be *Englisch* and go to Hell, if you have a heart of unbelief."

"So, are you saying that it really doesn't matter if a person is Amish or *Englisch*?"

"That's exactly what I'm saying. But some remain Amish, even if they have been saved by believing in Christ, because they know that if they don't, they will lose fellowship with their loved ones." He took a sip of his soda. "And then there are those who leave the Amish because they can't keep silent about what God has done in their hearts. If they remain Amish and speak about it, then they are shunned anyway. So, instead of enduring the hardships of Amish culture, they find freedom to practice their beliefs among the *Englisch*."

"This is what you have done, *jah*?"

"Yes, this is why I have remained *Englisch*. But I originally left for different reasons. My belief in Christ came as a result of leaving, so I thank God that He called me and opened my eyes to the truth."

"I can't leave. I have Tabitha and the *boppli* coming."

"Danny, you don't have to leave the Amish to get saved. Remember what we read? You can be saved by simply placing your faith—that heart knowledge we talked about—in Christ. All you have to do is call on Him and He promises to save you. That's why He died on the cross—to save you from your sins so you don't have to go to Hell. I don't know whether your friend is in Hell or not, but *you* don't have to go there. Tabitha and your *boppli* don't have to go there."

"I don't want to go there, Elam. I want to believe in Jesus."

"That's *gut*. *Sehr gut!*" Elam had a difficult time containing his excitement. "Just call on Him and ask Him to save you. There are no special words to say. He is listening to what is in your heart."

"Okay. I will right now." Danny smiled.

"Another thing." Danny looked to Elam before exiting his truck. "Will you come with me to Marlin's funeral? I know everyone will blame me for his death, and I probably deserve that. But I don't want to be there alone."

"Won't *Mamm* and *Daed* be there?"

"*Jah.* But I want you there. *You* understand, Elam."

Elam nodded. "Okay. Call me and let me know when it is. I'll be there."

"*Denki*, Elam. You've been a *gut* brother to me."

Elam now watched as Danny walked with new confidence toward the house that held so many memories for him. Memories that would be ingrained in his mind for as long as he lived, he supposed.

He breathed a silent prayer of thanks for the wondrous things that had transpired today. Danny was not only a brother through their biological blood, but now he was a brother by God's blood as well.

SIXTEEN

*A*ttending Marlin's funeral had brought back all the reasons Elam had for hating them. It all seemed so dark and hopeless, and he realized that for many of the people there—perhaps most, even—it was. Knowing you had Heaven awaiting you when you died was truly a gift, and each new circumstance seemed to remind Elam how precious that gift was.

He and Danny had stayed at the cemetery long after those in the community had gone. They discussed things they now had in common. It was peculiar that a tragic event for one person, could turn into a glorious opportunity for another. But that was how God worked—He could turn unfathomable tragedies into unbelievable blessings.

Elam looked around at the headstones, carefully reading each one. "Do you know where Julianna Yoder's marker is? I'd like to see it."

"Hmm...don't know." He surveyed the grave markers around him. "You know, it's strange that I don't remember attending her funeral."

"Maybe you didn't," Elam suggested.

"Do you want to check every one of these?"

"Not the ones we know have been here for ages. Just the more recent ones." They continued their search, examining each headstone.

"I don't see it anywhere."

"Could they have buried her somewhere else?"

"This is the only Plain cemetery in the area. She's gotta be here somewhere."

While Elam wanted to see Julianna's grave, a part of him hoped he wouldn't find it. If he did, he'd have to acknowledge something he hadn't allowed his heart to truly believe—that Julianna was indeed gone from this life. And that he would never see her again.

When Elam dropped his brother back off at their folks' house, he noticed extra buggies in the yard. No doubt, the leaders had come to reprimand them. He wondered if his recent presence had stirred up more trouble for them. He sincerely hoped not.

"*Ach*, it's Tabitha's folks and the deacon." Sheer dread filled Danny's voice and expression.

"Well, perhaps now would be a *gut* time to express your desire to get hitched."

"*Jah*. Now I regret not telling *Mamm* and *Daed* sooner. It will be more difficult for them if everyone is here." Danny opened the door to the truck and stepped out.

"Looks like you have no choice. God speed, *bruder*."

"*Denki*. Please say a prayer for us."

"I will do that. Remember, you can talk to me anytime. You know where I live and you have my number."

Danny nodded.

Elam pulled out of the driveway breathing out the prayer he'd just promised his brother. He added an extra request— that God would give him favor with Martha so he could find the answers he sought about Julianna. Mainly, where had she been buried?

Less than ten minutes later, he drove up to the property owned by Martha Yoder's family. Elam couldn't believe his eyes. Martha stood near the mailbox out by the road. Had *Der Herr* prompted her to take a walk at just the right time Elam drove by? Surely, God was already giving him favor.

A renewed confidence gave Elam the extra boost of determination he needed. God would help him.

Elam rolled down his passenger side window. "Hello, Martha."

"Elam, right?" Her cheeks darkened just a bit and Elam didn't know whether he'd just startled her or if she found him attractive. Hopefully, it was just the former. His life was already complicated enough.

"Yep, that's right. How are you doing?" He smiled.

"I'm doing *gut*." Curiosity danced in her eyes.

He'd better just get to the point while he had the chance.

"Will you tell me where Julianna's grave is? I searched every grave in the Amish cemetery, but I couldn't find it anywhere."

Martha frowned. "I...I can't help you."

"Why not, Martha? I don't think it is against the Amish rules to tell someone where a gravesite is. Right?"

She gave a wary smile. "I don't know if they want me to say anything."

"Why wouldn't they? It's a pretty simple request."

"There's no gravestone for her there." The words flew from her mouth, and she seemed to immediately regret them.

What? Elam's arm hairs suddenly stood on end. "I don't understand, Martha. How can she not have a gravestone? Is she buried someplace else?"

"Just a minute."

Elam watched in confusion as Martha turned and bolted to the house. What on earth was she doing? Was she going to get one of her brothers or her father so they could expel him from their property? He briefly contemplated leaving. A couple of moments later, Martha walked back out to the truck. She stuck her hand into the open truck window and thrust a folded piece of paper toward him.

He opened the paper and read what was written inside. It looked like an address. "What is this, Martha?"

"You can find her there." With that, Martha turned and briskly walked back to the house.

SEVENTEEN

*T*he moment he pulled in to his garage, Elam whipped out his phone and punched the address Martha had given him into the internet search engine.

He expected the name of a cemetery to show on his screen, but what appeared instead blew his mind. He frowned. *This can't be!*

Elam looked down at his phone screen and read it again. *Raven Street Psychiatric Hospital.* He shook his head. *I don't understand this, Lord. Why did Martha give me this address?* Perhaps she'd written down the wrong one? Maybe it was a mistake.

He dialed the phone number provided by the website. Perhaps Julianna had left the Amish and now worked at this place. *Jah,* that had to be it.

Someone at the other end of the line greeted him.

Elam cleared his throat. "Is there a Julianna Yoder working there?"

The woman paused. "Nobody by that name works here. I'm sorry."

Elam frowned. "Then do you have a *patient* there by the name of Julianna Yoder?"

"Who is calling?" the female voice answered.

"I am a friend of Julianna's."

"I'm sorry. We're not allowed to disclose that information over the phone."

"You can't even tell me whether she's there or not?" He couldn't help his incredulous tone.

"One moment, please."

The line went silent and Elam assumed the woman had put him on hold. He took a deep breath and silently prayed while he waited for what seemed like an eternity.

The woman came back on the line. "Yes, there is a patient here by the name of Julianna Yoder, but I can't provide any other information."

"Thank you." Elam clicked off the phone.

He wasn't even exactly sure what a psychiatric hospital was, but it didn't sound good. He picked up his phone again and typed in psychiatric hospital. Several institutions in the area came up with driving directions for each one. But that wasn't the information he needed. He wanted to know what went on inside one of these hospitals. *What had Julianna gone through these last couple of years?*

The results culminated from his online search did not provide him with the relief he sought. As a matter of fact, his anxiety now shot through the roof. Horrible photos of mistreated patients caused his heart to ache. He prayed this was not true of Julianna. Surely, mental institutions were more humane in this day and age. *Please, God. Please keep Julie safe.*

He checked the website again for visiting hours. It was too late to go today, but first thing tomorrow, he'd be on his way. He needed to check on Julianna. He needed assurance that she was okay.

Elam's hands clammed up as he pulled up to the psychiatric institution. The large brick building felt overwhelming and a bit intimidating. He couldn't imagine how Julianna survived here all alone, without the family and community that had surrounded her from birth.

He parked in the visitors section and whispered a prayer before exiting his vehicle. He had a feeling this visit would take all the strength he could muster, and an extra dose of supernatural strength would be greatly needed.

Elam frowned in disappointment as he entered the building through one of the two glass doors. He stood in an empty foyer, which contained a couple benches and an intercom system. He read the note next to the intercom system. *Push button. State who you are and your purpose.*

"Hello. My name is Elam Zook, and I'm here to visit Julianna Yoder." He felt a little silly talking into the device.

A voice returned. "What was the name of the patient?"

He pushed the button again. "Julianna Yoder. She's Amish."

"And your name?"

Elam sighed. "Elam Zook," he stated as slowly and clearly as possible.

"I'm sorry, sir. You are not on the list of visitors for this patient."

"List? But I drove an hour and a half to get here. And I took off work."

"A visit must be approved."

"By whom?"

"Her paperwork shows a visit must be approved by either Obadiah Yoder or Mose Hershberger."

Elam felt like slamming his head against a wall. "Does it need to be in writing? Do you require a phone call, or what?"

"Either a visit from one of them or a letter will be sufficient."

"Okay. Thank you." Elam scowled as he stomped back to his truck.

How on earth would he be able to get permission from Julianna's father or Bishop Hershberger? He couldn't see either one of them approving his visit. Now, if he were still Amish, they'd probably pounce on the opportunity for a single male, potential suitor to visit her in hopes of them marrying. But he wasn't Amish, and he had no desire to rejoin his former Amish district.

He sat in his truck and thought for a moment. If he only

knew who was on the list. If he did, then perhaps he could tag along with them. But even then, the administrators probably wouldn't allow him to see Julie.

If he knew how Bishop Hershberger or Obadiah Yoder wrote, he could possibly forge a handwritten letter. He frowned. *No, that would be dishonest. And most likely against the law.*

He bowed his head. *God, I need some help here. Please show me what to do.*

TRY AGAIN.

"Okay, Lord." He closed the door to his truck and walked back toward the building.

"Elam Zook? Is that you?" A voice called as a uniformed officer approached him. He guessed the person to have just exited the building.

"Yes." He smiled in recognition. "Randall Harris! How are you?"

"I'm great, as you can see. Are you on the force?"

Elam shook his head. "No. I changed my major—or my mind, rather. I have a cousin who served in the military and suffered PTSD and lost his leg as a result. That kind of deterred me from chasing a career as a peace officer. He comes from the same background I do, so I figured I might not do well."

"Hey, we all have our calling. Not everyone is cut out for this kind of profession. I've even questioned myself a time or two." Randall looked around. "What are you doing here, man?"

"I came to visit a friend, but I guess I'm not on the visitors list. They wouldn't allow me to enter."

The officer grimaced. "Yeah, they're pretty strict around here. Don't want any wackos coming in." He looked toward the entrance. "Let me see what I can do."

"Really?" A bolt of excitement shot through him.

"No promises, brother, but I'll try. Come on." He beckoned Elam back into the building they'd exited. Elam followed Randall as he used his card to bypass the intercom system and access the main entrance. They walked toward a service desk and the woman in attendance frowned when she noticed Elam at the officer's side.

"Officer Harris, what may I do for you?" She smiled politely.

Randall turned to him and asked who he wished to see. "Julianna Yoder, please."

"I'll have an attendant bring her to the main visiting area. You may meet her there." The woman picked up a telephone and spoke with someone, whom Elam guessed was on the other side of the door leading to the patients' residences.

"Thank you very much, Melissa." Randall nodded.

He then led him to the community visiting area she'd mentioned.

"Thank you so much, Randall. You don't know how much this means to me."

"Hey, anytime I can help out a friend. I know you're a good guy and you're not about to take off with a patient, hurt them, or bring them drugs. That's their main concern. Gotta keep the patients safe, you know?"

Elam smiled. "Sure."

"Okay, man, I gotta go now. I'll make sure your name gets added to the visitors list so you won't have this problem next time."

"I really appreciate that." He shook Randall's hand and watched in disbelief as his friend left.

Elam could not believe this. He knew it was God who had placed Randall there at just the right time so their paths would cross, just as He had yesterday with Martha. He hadn't seen his friend since his college days, yet here he was.

God, You are so good to me! Thank you.

EIGHTEEN

Elam stared out the window while he waited for the attendant to bring Julianna out. His nerves felt all jumbled up inside and he tried to calm himself by taking deep breaths as Megan had suggested when they'd had their first dance session.

The door opened and he turned to see an attendant escorting a woman in a wheelchair. But it wasn't Julianna. He turned back to the window and took another calming breath.

"Mr. Zook," the attendant called his name.

"Yes?" He turned around again.

She gestured to the woman. "Julianna Yoder."

He stared at the woman in the wheelchair. Her hair was the same color as Julianna's, but she seemed so different. This young woman was older than Julianna and weighed considerably more.

He swallowed and took a few steps closer. "Julianna?"

She brought her gaze to his, and this was when he finally found a recognizable trait. Her sparkling hazel-green eyes—

yet they seemed to have lost their sparkle. This was indeed Julianna. His Julianna.

He held his emotions in check as best as he could, but inside he felt like breaking down.

"Julianna, it's me. Elam." Perhaps he should have shaved his goatee, so he would be more recognizable.

She stared toward the window, but said nothing.

He looked to the attendant, who still stood behind the wheelchair. "May I?" He gestured toward the chair.

The attendant nodded then walked to one of the chairs and sat down with a magazine.

Elam wheeled Julianna over to one of the windows. "It's a nice day today, isn't it?" He looked to see if she'd respond, but there was nothing. No sound, as if she no longer had a voice.

He turned to the attendant who had brought Julianna out into the visiting area. "Does she speak?"

"She speaks when she wants to," the woman replied.

Elam nodded in understanding and the attendant went back to reading.

Elam crouched down in front of Julianna and took one of her hands between both of his. "Julianna, I know you remember me. Will you speak to me?"

She sighed and looked away.

"Are you upset with me?" He waited to see if she'd respond, but she didn't. "Julianna, I want to apologize. I know I said some things to you, things that hurt you. I wish

I could take them back. I wish I hadn't said them."

She continued to stare toward the window, a frown on her face.

Elam stood directly in front of her and met her eyes. "Will you forgive me, Julie?"

She suddenly blinked, as though she recognized him for the first time.

"Julie, it's me. It's Elam Zook."

She stared at him now and tears filled her eyes then spilled over. "Elam."

He wanted to hold her in his arms, to tell her everything would be okay. But, would it?

"Yes, Julie. It's Elam." Instead, he stroked her hand. "I've been living in the *Englisch* world. I just found out that you were here. If I would have known, I would have visited sooner."

He wouldn't say that he'd been told she was dead. Somehow, it didn't seem like that would be a comforting thought to someone who might be mentally ill. Or anybody, for that matter.

Elam still had a hundred questions. Why was Julianna here? What did she do that caused the leaders to believe she was in need of mental health care? Perhaps he could get answers from those who worked in this facility. Would they share any information with him?

"Julie, can you tell me why you're here?"

"No." Good. At least she was responding now.

"I want to help you, Julie. How can I help you?"

She shrugged.

He leaned close and whispered. "Would you like me to get you out?"

Her gaze fixed on him and sadness flashed across her features. She nodded.

"I'll try, but it might take some time. You'll need to be patient. We'll trust God."

The attendant approached. "Time is up."

Elam glanced up at her. "May we say goodbye?"

"Sure," the attendant muttered and turned around.

Elam leaned close to Julianna and held her, although a bit awkwardly because of her wheelchair. "I won't forget you, Julie."

The attendant turned and wheeled Julianna back out the door she'd brought her in from. Elam stared at the door a couple of moments before leaving through another exit.

He swallowed his emotion. Seeing Julie in this condition had been one of the most difficult things he'd ever experienced. *Please be with her, God.*

He made his way back to the front desk. The woman who'd been there earlier was now gone. On lunch break, he assumed. Another woman had taken her place.

"Excuse me, would you be able to tell me what Julianna was admitted for?" he asked, invoking his best smile.

She tapped on the computer keyboard in front of her. "Clinical Depression."

"And has she made any progress? Will she be able to be released soon?"

She peered at him over the frames of her glasses. "And you are?"

"A close friend." He smiled.

"I'm sorry, that information can only be discussed with her legal guardian."

"Okay. Thank you for your help, ma'am."

NINETEEN

The drive back home for Elam seemed to fly by. He'd been so deep in thought, he was unsure how he even got from point A to point B. But somehow, he'd made it home.

Everything within him wanted drive back to Raven Street Psychiatric Hospital and rescue Julianna. What he would do with her after that, he hadn't a clue. Not that he would ever have that opportunity. He didn't have the authority to release her.

What he needed was answers. How could he help Julianna fight her depression? What could he do to facilitate healing in her life? He'd never studied medicine, so he was clueless. But it seemed like whatever drugs they'd put her on at the hospital were not working. That was evident to even him.

God, please direct me.

He picked up his Bible and began reading. Proverbs was where one went to get wisdom, and that was exactly what he needed. The Bible held the answers to everything, right? So why not look for wisdom on Julianna's condition?

After reading and studying God's Word for a couple of hours, Elam came to at least one conclusion he already knew. Julianna needed Christ in her life. Because if she knew how precious she was in God's eyes, he was certain that fact alone would give her the boost of self-worth she craved.

Julianna watched out the window as Elam entered a red truck and left. She'd wanted to say more to him, to ask him the many questions zooming through her mind at the moment, but they couldn't seem to come out. Her brain was so *ferhoodled.*

First, she hadn't recognized this *Englisch* stranger. Once she realized who he was, she'd been confused as to why he was there. What did he want?

When they'd last parted, his words to her had been harsh. But she had deserved them. She knew that. His words had stayed with her and had played in her head hundreds of times over the past few years. She'd been so upset and angry over them. Elam's verbal betrayal had stung even more than their actual breakup.

And then he'd left. He'd left for the *Englisch* world. Instead of staying and fighting for their relationship, instead of standing up to her father, he'd thrown in the towel. She wasn't worth it. She hadn't been worth his effort, his time, his love. This, she knew to be truth.

But now he was back. Why?

"Danny, I need a favor from you." Did Elam's voice sound as desperate as he felt? He sighed through the phone. "I found Julianna."

"Where was she buried? I thought we'd checked every headstone."

"She's not dead, Danny. She's in a mental institution."

"What? You're kidding."

"No, I'm not. That's why I need a favor from you."

"What do you need, Elam?"

"I need answers. I want to know how she ended up there."

"I don't know how I can help you. I'm not exactly in good standing right now."

Elam heard a crackling sound and figured his brother was fiddling with the phone cord. He remembered doing the same in years past. It seemed like the phone shanty down the road from his folks' place probably had the same phone that had been there for at least twenty years. Since he'd been *Englisch*, he'd owned at least three different cell phones. It would probably seem silly to most *Englischers*, but it was little things like this that made him long for the simple comforts of Plain life.

"Do you know her brother?"

"Mark Yoder? *Jah.*"

"Could you fish around? See if you can get some answers?"

"I'll try. I can ask Tabitha if she's heard anything too."

"Oh, good. *Denki*, Danny." Elam nodded although no one saw him. "By the way, how did your confrontation go?

"*Mamm* cried when she found out. Tabitha and I are getting married next month. *Daed* insisted."

"That's *gut*. Where will you live?"

"With her folks until I can earn enough money to get us a place of our own."

"I have no doubt you can make it work."

"*Denki*, Elam."

"Call me when you get any information, okay?"

"You got it." The phone clicked off. Amish never were much for long goodbyes.

TWENTY

Clam pushed the bar from his chest for the fiftieth time, if he'd counted right, knowing he could easily add more weight to it if Zach were here to spot for him. But he didn't feel like having company right now. He needed this peaceful and quiet activity to try to sort out his thoughts.

His mind kept going back to Julianna, just sitting there in the wheelchair. Did she ever get any exercise? Surely the workers at the psychiatric hospital knew how important it was for their patients to get proper exercise and fresh air and sunshine.

He still couldn't get over how different she looked. If he hadn't been told and hadn't gotten close enough, he wouldn't even have recognized her. She'd changed so much— seemingly in every way. She appeared to be melancholy, or almost in a daze even. He'd been startled to see her in such a state.

Although she looked different on the outside, he knew that she had to be the same person on the inside. Perhaps she was buried in loneliness from being in that place. Perhaps it was the medications they had her on that hid her inner person.

He wished he knew how she felt. He wished that she could express it so he could know how to help her. He'd asked her if she wanted him to try to get her released and she'd responded positively. Did she fully understand what he was asking? Now, he wondered if it had been wise to utter those words. What if he failed? What if he wasn't able to rescue her? What if he'd given her false hope and only caused her condition to worsen?

He slid his ankles under the leg bar and completed his usual exercise routine. After he finished, he planned to take Scramble over to the school and run a few miles on the track, before returning for a shower.

His phone buzzed and he answered right away. "Hello?"

"Hi, Elam."

He blew out a breath and smiled. "Megan. It's good to hear your voice."

"Yours too." There was a short period of silence. "Uh, are you still planning on picking me up?"

"Picking you…" *Oh, shoot. Do I have a date scheduled with Megan?* He stared at his phone, but the time didn't show. "What time is it?"

"A quarter till. We're supposed to go bowling with the singles class tonight, remember?"

He frowned. No, he didn't remember. "A quarter till what?"

"Six."

"Six?" How on earth had the last two hours just slipped away? He'd been so preoccupied with thoughts of Julie, the outing with his singles class totally slipped his mind. He sighed. "Megan, I'm not even close to being ready. I just finished my workout and planned to take Scramble out for a run. Would you be terribly disappointed if I bailed on you?"

Silence reigned for a few seconds. "No, I guess not." He heard the disappointment in her voice.

"Sorry."

"No, it's okay. Elam, is everything all right?"

"Yep. Everything's fine. I'll see you tomorrow morning at church, okay?"

"Okay. Goodbye."

Elam blew out an extended breath and tucked his phone into the pocket of his shorts. As much as he hated to disappoint Megan, he looked forward to a quiet evening alone. He had a few things he needed to figure out.

He opened the back door and clipped Scramble's leash to his collar. "Come on, boy. Let's go for a jog."

Elam stared at his busted up motorcycle and wondered if it was even salvageable. A tow truck had dropped it off just a few minutes ago. It now stood in his garage as a monument to his foolishness. Why had he agreed to let his brother borrow it? What if it had been his brother that had died?

Yep, he would need to get rid of it. The sooner, the better.

TWENTY-ONE

"Elam? It's about time you showed up. It's been, what, two weeks since you last visited?"

Elam stared at Zach. "I know. But I've been so busy, the time has flown by."

Rosanna stepped into the room with snacks in hand, two whoopie pies for each of them and mugs of steaming black coffee. This was one thing he loved about his Amish roots. One could show up at any time and most folks would stop what they were doing to wait on you, welcome you, and sit and visit with you—as though you were the most important thing in the world at the moment.

Zach pointed at him. "You've been keeping secrets. I can tell."

"You can?"

"Yes. Spill it." Zach laced his fingers together and cracked his knuckles.

"I went to see Julianna." Elam sipped his coffee.

"You said she was in some mental hospital, right?"

Elam nodded. "Yeah, she is."

"And?"

"And, I'm not sure exactly what to do."

"About?" Zach bit into his whoopie pie.

"I hate seeing her there, Zach. I want to get her out."

"Why is she there?"

"I'm not *exactly* sure, but the 'official' diagnosis from the hospital states 'clinical depression.' I'd be depressed if I had to be there too."

Zach nodded. "I can certainly relate to that. I went through a lot of depression, guilt, and self-pity after returning from Afghanistan. I still feel bouts of it at times."

"So what helped you break free of that?"

"Number one—I got saved. That was monumental in helping me overcome it. But having Rosanna and Frank and Betty are a real blessing. And my little ones. It's difficult to be sad when I look at all the blessings I still do have. I'm surrounded by God's goodness every day."

Elam frowned. What blessings did Julie have that she could see? It seemed a place like that would only make her feel worse—especially since she was Amish and used to having family and community all around her.

"I have to get her out of there, Zach."

"And how do you plan to do that?"

"That's what I've been trying to figure out. Got any ideas?"

"Not particularly. But, if it helps, Rosanna and I could go visit her."

Elam shook his head. "You have to be on the visitors list. Her father and the bishop are the ones who control it, so that's pretty much out of the question."

"How'd *you* see her, then?"

Elam's face brightened. "That was a miracle in itself. God got me in. I prayed, and He made a way. I ran into an old friend that I'd taken criminal justice classes with when I was in college. Apparently, he works at the hospital from time to time. He used his privileges to get me in and put me on the list."

"Wow. It's sounds as though you don't need my help. Why don't you pray and ask God to show you what to do?"

"That's a good idea. But any advice you might have wouldn't hurt either."

"I don't know if I have any. But I am curious what will happen to her once she leaves. Will she have the support she needs? Is there someone in the community who will help her get back on her feet? Would she return to her folks' place? If they did indeed send her away because of depression, what is going to keep her from slipping back into that pit? You do realize that depression can easily lead to suicide, right? These are all questions you'll need the answers to."

Elam blew out a noisy breath. "I hadn't considered those things."

"Those things will need to be determined *before* she is released. Maybe she's in an institution because it's the safest place for her. Have you considered that?"

"I can't imagine that would be true. She was so...*normal* before."

Zach shrugged. "People change."

Elam thought back to the Julianna he'd known in the past compared to the one that now sat in a psychiatric institution. Yep, she'd definitely changed.

Danny's voice crackled on the other end of the line. "I found out some information. I'm not sure if it's anything you can use though."

"What did you find out, Danny?"

"Well, I talked to Tabitha, who talked to her sister Joanna, who's *gut* friends with Julianna's cousin Martha, who talks to Julianna's sister."

Elam squeezed his eyes closed and tried to make the connection in his mind. "Okay, Martha."

"Well, Julianna's sister Naomi told Martha, who told Joanna, who told Tabitha, who told me that shortly after Cletus Stolzfoos stopped courting Julianna, she quit attending singings and just stayed home."

"And?"

"That's all I found out."

"Oh." His bubble of excitement burst. "*Why* did she stop going to singings?"

"It seems like she did ride home with a couple of other

boys, but it didn't seem to work out." He paused. "I heard tell that maybe she had a reputation."

"*What?*"

"You know."

"No, I *don't* know. If it's what I'm thinking, Julianna was *not* like that."

"Maybe just not with *you*."

Elam felt like he might have steam blowing out of his ears. He clenched his hands at his sides. It was a good thing he was using the speaker phone, otherwise his cell might be crushed.

"I don't know, brother. That's just what I heard."

Elam took a calming breath. "Anything else you can think of?"

"Um, now that you mention it, I think she may have mentioned something about jumping the fence."

Elam scratched his head. "Who? Me?"

"No, Julianna talked about it to her sister Naomi or maybe her cousin."

"And?"

"Seems she never did. Just talked about it is all."

Elam heard giggling come through the other line. "Danny? You still there?"

"*Jah*, I'm here. I should probably go though. Seems Tabitha might want a *buss*."

Elam clicked off the phone, but not before hearing a gasp of mock exasperation. He shook his head but smiled, partially envying his brother.

He remembered a time in the not-so-distant past when he and Julianna would sneak out and meet at the phone shanty to share a secret kiss or two. So much had changed since that time in their lives. Some things were better, like his introduction to Christ. But other things were far worse.

Hopefully, *those* things would be changing soon.

TWENTY-TWO

Each time Elam visited with Julianna, his heart ached. He couldn't keep doing this. At least not without trying to get her released. He still had no clue how to make that possible.

Many times, he'd entertained thoughts of contacting the bishop or Julianna's father. And each time he reminded himself that he was an outsider—and possibly a threat to their lifestyle. Why *would* they listen to him? They wouldn't, not unless he had a plan in place that would benefit Julianna, her family, and the community.

He sighed, and prayed again. He'd just read a passage in the Bible about not planning what to say beforehand, but letting God put the words in your mouth. He knew that this would be taking the verse out of context, but he did desire to rescue Julianna and see her saved. And he was all out of ideas on how to make it work. But God had helped him before and Elam was confident that He would now.

He prayed once again for the boldness he needed.

Elam leaned forward in the chair and locked eyes with Bishop Hershberger. "I'd like to ask permission to release Julianna Yoder from the institution."

"You have had contact with her?" The bishop frowned.

"Uh, limited contact, yes."

"Does she appear to have recovered from her illness?"

"Illness? But I thought…" What *did* he think? He knew Julie had been sent away, but he was unaware of what exactly the reasoning was, as far as the elders were concerned. Was he referring to her depression?

"Her obstinate ways. Is she willing to forsake them?" The bishop clarified.

This was not the conversation he'd expected. *Her obstinate ways? Did they send her away because she was misbehaving according to their desired rules of conduct? Was it because of the rumors Danny had mentioned? Or was this about the fact that she'd mentioned jumping the fence?* Whatever it was, it seemed the main reason for sending her away was not about depression.

Fury raged in Elam's veins as he realized what this man was implying, but he did his best to hide his true feelings. He must remain cool if he was to win any favor with the bishop. If he had any chance of him approving her release. *Help me remain calm, Lord.*

"I…I'm not sure. We didn't exactly discuss that."

Bishop Hershberger raised a doubtful brow. "She is better off there than out in the world. If it is the world she seeks, she must remain in the institution. We sent her to a *good* place, not one that seeks to convert patients to modern Christianity."

It took all of Elam's resolve not to burst out in anger. How could he deny her the peace that came from knowing the Saviour? How could this man have such control over another human being? He knew it was a good thing he'd left when he did, but would there have been a different outcome for Julianna if he'd stayed and spoken up? He couldn't bide the thought of Julie being mistreated. "What would it take for Julianna to be released?"

"Released?" The bishop's brow shot up. Had he not heard his initial request?

"Yes. I don't think she's getting the help she needs there. She's despondent and hardly speaks."

"She must agree to the ways of our people. She must agree to become baptized and devote her life to our ways. We would not want her to go to Hell." His demeanor was totally serious.

There was no way that Julianna would've agreed to that if she had been anything like him when he left. There was nothing that was going to keep him in the community. But he doubted that Julianna had the fortitude to fight for anything right now—which was the reason he was here, to be her voice. Living amongst the Amish wasn't the worst thing in the world, and it was definitely preferable to being locked up in a psychiatric hospital.

He eyed the bishop now. He didn't trust him. He certainly had no interest in letting Julianna live under the watchful eye of the leadership here, but what choice was there? He had to come up with a foolproof plan—one they couldn't refuse.

Please help me, Lord. Give me wisdom to do the right thing.

The bishop continued. "She needs to marry and settle down, but she is an *alt maedel* now and I fear no Plain man would want her. Especially with her...*issues.*"

Elam's heart began racing. He knew what he must do now. *Could* he do this? Could he go through with a plan that defied all logic and common sense? For Julianna's sake, he had to.

"I have a solution. It will keep her here for *gut.*" He took a deep breath and wiped his sweaty palms on his jeans. He swallowed, then met the bishop's eyes. "I'll make a kneeling confession and rejoin the church, then I'll marry Julianna."

Bishop Hershberger's eyes widened, then he nodded in obvious approval. "*You* wish to marry her?" It was apparent he considered Julianna to be past all hope of marriage and having a family.

"I do." He strengthened his resolve, and did his best not to question himself. "The reason I left in the first place was because I'd thought she would marry someone else. I couldn't stand to see that." It *was* partially true.

"How do I know this isn't a trick? What assurance can you give me?"

"Bishop Hershberger, if I become Amish again and marry Julianna, I will be making a huge sacrifice. I presently own two vehicles—a truck and a motorcycle. I will have to sell those. I also have a house. And an *Englisch* girlfriend, I might add. I will be giving up a lot." *I'm sorry, Megan.*

The bishop examined Elam, a flicker of reticence in his eye. "You would give these things up and become Amish again?" He repeated, most likely to be sure he was hearing Elam correctly.

Elam grimaced inwardly. "I would."

Mose Hershberger's countenance brightened significantly. "Very well, then. I will make a phone call tomorrow. And *you* will take care of those things you mentioned, I presume?"

Elam nodded, regret already seeping in at the realization of what he just offered the bishop.

Question after question buzzed in Elam's mind like a swarm of bees around a hive. What was he going to tell Megan? How would he explain to her that he'd just agreed to marry another woman—after *they'd* been dating for several months?

Was Julianna even *willing* to marry him? Did she want to come back to the community where everyone would be talking about her? For all he knew, she might not want to have anything to do with him. After all, she'd been the one who ended their relationship. By no means did he want to force her into doing something she didn't wish to do. And what of Julie's folks? They'd seemed dead set against their relationship in the past. Would they approve of this ridiculous notion?

He blew out a long breath and prayed he was making the right decision. Because any way this scenario played out, lives would be changed forever. *God, I need your strength.*

TWENTY-THREE

Elam raked his hand through his hair. He'd never second-guessed himself so much in his life. "I don't know what I'm doing, Zach! Have I lost my sanity?"

"I'm sorry, Elam, but I have no idea how to help you." Zach frowned. "Sometimes, the right thing to do seems like the wrong thing and vice versa."

"What?"

"I don't know. It's just...when Rosanna came into my life, I wanted nothing more than to get to know her—to court her. I just *knew* she was the one for me. I fell for her hard. But when I saw that John was thinking of leaving the Amish, I couldn't imagine life without my best friend. He showed an interest in Rosanna and I knew that if he fell in love with her, he'd stay. It was a tough decision, because I knew that I could probably win Rosanna's heart if I pursued her. So I did what I thought was the unselfish thing—whether the right or wrong thing, I don't know—and I stepped out of the way. And you know how the rest of our story goes."

"I'm sure that was tough."

"The hardest thing I've ever done. We've gone through so much, but each trial has made us stronger."

"I sure never thought I'd go back to the Amish."

Zach chuckled. "And I never dreamed I'd become *Englisch.* You just never know what's going to come next in this crazy life. Just be true to your heart—do what God is telling you is the right thing, even though it may carry great risk. It might just bring the greatest reward you never imagined could be possible." Zach looked pointedly at Elam.

"I just don't know how I'm going to break the news to Megan."

"Do you love Megan?"

Elam shrugged. "How does one determine something like that? I mean, I enjoy spending time with her. And she's really sweet."

"Okay, let me put it this way. If you were to break things off with her right now, would her memory be greater to you than any other woman?"

Elam grimaced.

"Is that a 'no'?"

"It's not that I don't care for her. I do. But I don't know if anyone's memory can surpass Julianna. I feel like I left most of my heart with her. I would have married her in a heartbeat. I just felt like I had this connection with her that I've never felt with anyone else."

"Then it sounds like you may have your answer."

A voice came from the kitchen and both Zach and Elam looked up. "What's this about getting married? Elam Zook, is there something you haven't told me?"

"Oh, hi, Grandma Brooks." He stood up and gave the woman a hug. Although they called her 'Grandma,' she was closer in age to his parents.

Frank and Betty Brooks had taken Zachariah in after he returned from the war, broken in both body and soul. They had lost their own son, Tommy, in that same conflict in the Middle East. It was through them that Zach had come to Christ and eventually recovered from his PTSD, although he still occasionally had to fight falling back into depression from the flashbacks. But having loved ones nearby helped immensely in dealing with the past and recognizing his sense of purpose in life once again.

"Are you thinking of marrying Miss Megan? I hear you two have been seeing an awful lot of each other lately."

Elam grimaced. "No, someone else, actually."

"Oh, my. Now *this* I gotta hear." Grandma Brooks planted herself down on the sofa next to Elam and patted his knee. "Poor Miss Megan. The way that girl looks at you, I can tell she's smitten."

Elam took a deep breath. "It's kind of a sudden thing, yet not really. Okay, let me get you up to speed. Do you remember me talking about a girl named Julianna?"

Grandma Brooks shook her head. "Can't say I do. This old memory isn't what it used to be."

"Anyway, she's one of the reasons I left the Amish. She was my girlfriend for about a year until she broke up with me for another guy. I figured they'd gotten married and lived happily ever after.

"Well, I went back several months ago to satisfy my curiosity, I guess you can say. The wedding between the two of them never happened, and apparently, she never married anyone else. When I asked around of Julianna's whereabouts, I finally was informed that she had died."

Grandma Brooks gasped and touched Elam's hand. "Oh, dear. I'm so sorry, Elam."

Elam shook his head. "But here's the thing, Grandma Brooks, Julianna *didn't* die."

"What?"

"I know, it sounds crazy. And crazy is exactly what this whole thing is. It seems like Julianna had been going through quite a bit, emotionally speaking, and they didn't know how to help her—I really don't know the whole story yet, though—and they sent her away to a psychiatric hospital." He was certain the anger showed through his face each time he shared that bit of information with anyone. It was difficult to say the words, let alone picture Julianna sitting in a mental institution for years, all alone and amongst complete strangers. He could only imagine how frightened she must have been. He continued to ask himself, *What if I would have been there to protect her, to speak up for her? How different would her situation have been?*

"Anyway, the bishop or her father has to consent to her release. The bishop seems to be worried that she will leave the Amish, and he'd rather she stay at the institution than jump the fence."

Grandma Brooks frowned. "What?"

"I know it may not make much sense to outsiders, but as a former Amish man, I can *somewhat* understand where he is coming from—not that I agree with him in any way, shape or form. You see, to the Amish, if a member leaves the church, they believe they are doomed to most certain Hell. So, in the bishop's mind, Julianna being in an institution is preferable to Hell."

Grandma Brooks gasped.

"I went and spoke to the bishop, and he was surprisingly reasonable. I told him that I would rejoin the Amish, and marry Julianna. That would secure her future in the Amish church, thus saving both her and myself from impending Hell, in his eyes."

"And he agreed to this?"

"He did."

"And what did Julianna say? Have you spoken with her?"

"I have spoken with her, but not about marriage."

"This young lady, is she a believer?"

He read the concern in Grandma Brooks' countenance.

Elam shook his head. "I'm pretty sure she is not. I tried to speak with her about it, but her head is so muddled right now with all the medication they have her on. I don't think she understood a word." He felt like crying at the thought.

"The Bible speaks against being unequally yoked with non-believers."

"I do understand that…"

"I hear a 'but' coming next."

"But I can't help but think of certain stories in the Bible. Remember Hosea? God told *him* to marry a harlot."

Grandma Brooks laughed. "How many men have used that story out of context, I wonder?"

"Okay, I do know the context of the story of God's love toward Israel. But what about the theme of sacrifice? Isn't that what Hosea did? Isn't that what Jesus did? They laid down their lives for their bride.

"And God is not willing that any should perish, right? Julianna will certainly perish in body, soul, and spirit if she stays there, I'm certain of it. I know it's not a guarantee, but I'm almost positive that Julianna would accept Christ as her Saviour if given the opportunity. But where she is now, it's impossible. She barely speaks and she can't even think straight.

"I love her. I want to help her find her way back."

"And what if she doesn't accept Christ, then what?"

"Then I'll spend the rest of my life being the best husband and example I can be to try and win her."

She patted his hand. "I have no doubt that you will be, Elam. She would be blessed to have you as her husband. But, you are taking a great risk."

"I realize that."

"I'm guessing you haven't broken the news to Miss Megan yet."

"No, not yet. Please pray for me. For her."

"Oh, I do, honey. But I will add a few extra prayers in there."

"Thanks, Grandma Brooks. I really do appreciate it."

"I know you do, Elam." A sad look flashed in her eyes. "I guess that means we won't be seeing much of you anymore."

"Probably not, but I'll try to visit when I can."

"Zach still needs you as a friend, so don't be gone too long and visit often."

He nodded in understanding.

TWENTY-FOUR

*T*he clamminess of Elam's hands was only a minor annoyance as he sat in the midst of this group of men—Bishop Hershberger, Minister Zehr, Minister Borntreger, Deacon Schwartz, and Obadiah Yoder. He took his hat off and rotated it in his hands. It felt strange, yet not, to be dressed in Amish clothing once again. He'd shaven his goatee and done everything he could to gain the favor of this group and prove his sincerity. He'd left his truck at his folks' place and borrowed their buggy to attend this meeting.

He now looked at each one as they sat chatting—as though this wasn't one of the most pivotal occasions in his life. This was his moment of truth—the thing he'd been dreading and looking forward to both at the same time.

The bishop addressed the group, "As you know, Elam Zook has expressed a desire to rejoin our community and marry Julianna Yoder." He turned to Julianna's father. "Obadiah, you are agreeable to this, correct?"

"*Jah.*"

"I, too, feel this will be beneficial for our community and

for Julianna." The bishop looked at each of the men. "Do any of you have any questions or concerns?"

Deacon Schwartz nodded, his mien shrouded in suspicion. "He has been *Englisch* for several years now. How do we know he's not going to influence our young folks to embrace the *Englisch* ways?"

Elam spoke up, "I have no intentions of doing that. My desire is to marry Julianna, raise a family, and live a quiet and peaceable life amongst our people."

Minister Borntreger spoke now. "Will he have a time of proving?"

"We have yet to discuss that," Bishop Hershberger said. "I recommend sixty days. This will give Elam time to sell his worldly belongings and find a suitable home within the community."

Elam frowned. He'd hoped he would be exempted of a proving time. "Does it have to be sixty days? I'd hoped to have Julianna released as soon as possible."

"Julianna will be released to her father's care this week," the bishop assured.

Obadiah spoke up. "Once you get your affairs in order, you may begin courting her."

"Does anyone know of any property for sale?" Elam didn't have the money yet, but as soon as he sold his current home, he'd have a decent down payment.

"There's a few acres with a small house out on Cherry Ridge Road. It's just down from the school house a couple of miles." The deacon suggested.

"I don't know what you'll have in terms of cash, but there's a pretty nice piece of land across from the Stolzfoos ranch." Minister Zehr chimed in.

That was the last place he'd consider. And something he'd never be able to afford. He'd be insane to move across the street from Julianna's ex-boyfriend.

"Thank you. I'll contact my realtor and see if there are any other places as well." Elam nodded.

"You'll need to sell your vehicle as soon as possible. The sooner you embrace the ways of our people, the better." Bishop Hershberger met his gaze. "I assume you'll move into your folks' place for now?"

He knew the bishop's comment had not been a request but a command. Elam now had a dilemma. How would he go about getting to work every day?

"My job is in town and I'd hoped to live in the house until it is sold. Having a vehicle is necessary to—"

"So you *do not* wish to return to your Plain community then?"

"No, I—"

"Then you will find a way. Just like any other Amish man would. The sooner you embrace our ways, Elam, the lighter your burden will be."

He wanted to scoff at that comment. Every man present knew that the Amish did not carry a 'light' burden. No, being under a yoke of bondage and having a taskmaster over you was unpleasant at best. Would he truly be able to conform to the Amish ways after being free these last few years? For Julianna's sake, he had to.

"Okay. I will do what it takes." Elam sighed.

"*Gut.* I'd hoped you'd say that. You will make a kneeling confession in front of the congregation at the next meeting. Are you agreeable to this?"

"*Jah.*"

TWENTY-FIVE

Clam held Megan close as they swayed back and forth to the music. The aroma from her scented candles still tantalized his senses every time he was in her home. More than just a smidgen of regret filled his heart. This would most likely be the last time in her home—their last dance.

Somewhere along the line in their relationship, they'd stopped waltzing and employed slow dancing instead. This was easier and somehow more intimate. She leaned her head on his shoulder and turned to look at him. What usually came next was a kiss, but he couldn't offer one.

Not now.

She felt wonderful in his arms, but he could no longer do this. He *had to* tell her the truth. This beautiful woman he'd come to know and respect and care for would never be his life mate.

Guilt seeped in and anchored itself inside his soul. It wasn't fair, not to her or Julianna, considering what he'd promised Bishop Hershberger and the Amish leaders.

Julianna and he would be married soon, and dancing intimately with another woman—one who would never become his wife—suddenly felt wrong. It would be difficult, but he had to tell Megan everything.

He stopped dancing and pulled back.

Megan's eyes searched his. "Is something wrong, Elam?"

He sighed. "We need to talk."

Elam motioned toward the couch and they sat down. He took her hand in his and inhaled a deep breath. "Megan. You have been amazing. But there's something I need to tell you."

She nodded for him to continue. If she was worried, she didn't let on.

"Sheesh, I don't know how to say this. Let me start at the beginning."

"Okay."

"Remember how I told you that I used to be Amish? Well, I used to have an *aldi*—a girlfriend—but we broke up. I left not too long after that.

"Before you and I started dating, I went back to my community to see how Julianna was getting along and learned that she had passed away. Or, that's what I was led to believe. Anyway, I somewhat recently found out that she didn't die. She'd been hospitalized for...some problems."

He rushed through the rest. "To make a long story short, I asked to have her released. But the only way the bishop would agree to it is if she joined the church as a baptized member and got married."

This was the tough part. He locked eyes with Megan and grimaced. "I said that I would…" He swallowed hard. "That I would marry Julianna."

"Whoa, wait." Megan frowned and he could almost see thoughts of confusion running through her mind. "So, let me get this straight. You told the Amish bishop that *you* were going to marry *her*?"

He now detected tears in her eyes. How he hated causing other people pain—especially someone as sweet as Megan.

Elam hung his head. "Yes. And I'm rejoining the Amish."

"Elam, we've been dating for six months. Six months! When you said you wanted to talk, I was hoping you had in mind to propose or at least offer me a promise ring." She brushed away a few tears and Elam noticed her hands shaking. "I…I don't know what to say. I thought we had something special together."

"We did." He swallowed.

"Then why would you do this? Why would you ask somebody else to marry you?" Her quivering voice rose an octave. "Help me understand this, Elam! Tell me the truth. Is she pregnant with your baby?"

"Pregnant? No!"

"But you've been seeing her while we've been dating?"

"I have seen her a few times, yes." While he hadn't been dating Julianna, as he figured was Megan's thought, he didn't say it outright. Because if he were honest with himself, just seeing Julianna made him fall in love with her all over again. And that would be just as bad, if not worse, than dating her. She'd always be his true love, it was something he couldn't deny. Even if Megan was a wonderful person—even if her heart was most likely breaking right now.

"Great. I can't believe this. I really can't, Elam. I thought for sure you... I meet this *perfect* guy. Perfect. He's sweet, he's kind, a Christian, and my father even approves of him." She shot up from the couch and broke down in tears, his words fully registering in her mind no doubt.

"I'm sorry, Megan." He stood and attempted to pull her close, but she pushed him away.

"You're sorry? Just don't, Elam. I'd rather you just left now." She turned her back to him.

"Megan..." He reached to touch her shoulder then dropped his hand before making contact.

"Just *go*. *Please*. Don't make this any harder than it is."

He hated to leave her this way. He hated the fact that he seemed like a total jerk. But what option did he have? Megan could never understand. He had to try and reassure her. "It's nothing you did."

She nodded.

"I *do* care for you, Megan. Please don't think that I don't. That I didn't. My heart was invested in this relationship too."

A scornful laugh leapt from her lips and she spun around, demanding truth with her gaze. "Really, Elam? No, your heart was *not* invested in *me* at all. That's quite obvious."

"If there was another way..."

"You're acting like you have no control over this situation. *You* chose to see another woman while *we* were still dating. I call that unfaithfulness. *You—*"

"But I never—"

"Please let me finish, Elam." She huffed. "*You* are *choosing* to marry *her*. It seems to me like you're in total control of this situation. You're not a helpless bystander. If you *wanted* this to go another way, then that's what you would've chosen."

"Megan…" He should quit while he was ahead, or rather, behind. Really, there was nothing he could say to change the situation with Megan. He just felt terrible that she had to be the one to lose. He felt terrible that he was causing her this pain. He felt terrible that he was indeed choosing another woman over her, whether he felt justified or not. "I'm sorry."

Tears now poured down Megan's cheeks. "I don't understand why you would do this to me, Elam. Do you make it a habit of breaking hearts? Do you think that love is just some game?"

"No," he whispered. Seeing Megan's heartbreak now tore at his heart. He wished he could hold her one last time, and kiss away her tears. He wished he could somehow make things better. If he could have foreseen these events, he would have never begun a relationship with her in the first place. He would have spared her all this pain. But he couldn't, and he'd just have to trust that God had something better planned for both of them.

The way she'd spoken made him feel wicked, but what could he do? Julianna's very *life* was at stake. His thoughts catapulted back to the statistic he'd read online about there being twice as many deaths in psychiatric institutions in the past four decades than combined war deaths since 1776. Several millions. He couldn't let Julie be one of them. If he didn't rescue Julie, he was certain she'd die all alone in that retched place. And that was something he'd never forgive himself for.

He longed to tell Megan the whole truth. But somehow, he didn't think that telling her he was leaving her for someone in a mental institution would help the situation. It would only make her feel worse. So he kept silent. "I am truly sorry, Megan."

"Sorrow without repentance is meaningless. Goodbye, Elam." Megan shook her head, anguish written on her face, she then spun around and walked down the hall toward her bedroom.

Elam knew a part of his heart would remain with her. But like other painful chapters in his life, this one was now closed. Hopefully, the next chapter would bring better things—happier things. And, God willing, the last chapter would be the best one of all.

He had no doubt that Megan had a good cry after he left her house for the last time. And if he were honest, he'd admit that he did too.

TWENTY-SIX

*H*e hated this place.

Every time he was here, his heart ached with sadness. His only desire right now was to rescue Julianna. To protect her. To be what he should have been in the first place. Instead of facing things like a man, he'd run away to the *Englisch* world. It was true that good came as a result, but the truth remained. He'd failed Julianna. He wouldn't let that happen again.

"I'd like to take her for a walk outside in the garden. Is that okay?" He looked to the attendant.

"Yes, you may. She will be released soon anyway."

"Thank you." Elam placed the gift he'd brought into the bottom portion of Julianna's wheelchair. He wheeled her to the elevator and the three of them rode down to the main floor.

"It's this way." The attendant gestured to a side door.

They exited the building and the attendant took a seat on one of the garden benches, allowing them privacy. Elam was unsure why the attendant had escorted them out, because if they were worried about visitors escaping with the patients, then what was the purpose of the fence that lined the outskirts of the garden? Perhaps they stayed close in case the patients needed them. Elam didn't know.

"Are you enjoying the sunshine, Julie? It feels good, doesn't it?" He moved the footrests out of the way and took her hands. "Would you like to walk with me?"

At her nod, he helped her up. He placed his arm around her waist and noticed she was very weak. "Can you walk? We can sit on this bench up ahead if it's too much for you."

They walked the short way to the bench. Elam swallowed the lump in his throat. It was going to take a lot of time and effort to rehabilitate Julianna, but he was up to the task.

"Just a minute. I need to get something." Elam hurried to where he'd left the wheelchair and grabbed the gift he'd brought.

He placed it in her lap. "I brought you something. Will you open it?"

Her face brightened. "*Jah.*"

He watched as she slowly unwrapped the gift. He'd wanted to help her, but allowed her to take her time. When the wrapping paper had been removed, he helped her open the cardboard box. He carefully lifted out the wooden cuckoo clock.

"Do you like it?"

Her eyes lit up and the delight on her face was the best

show of positive emotion he'd seen from Julianna since he'd visited her in the institution. She stroked the clock with her hand and Elam read the question in her eyes.

"Yes, it is what you're thinking." He smiled and took her hand in his. "Julie, will you marry me?"

Tears sprung to her eyes and spilled over onto her cheeks. She smiled. "Yes, Elam."

She'd said his name! And she'd said yes! Elam took the clock from her lap and laid it to the side. He gathered her in his arms and gently kissed her lips. "I love you, Julie."

Julianna closed her eyes as the vehicle she traveled in moved toward her Amish community. She couldn't believe she was finally going home. Truly, she never thought she'd leave that place.

She had Elam to thank for all of this. Her heart swelled with gratitude for him. Her father had explained the entire situation to her. How Elam discovered that she was in the institution and went to the leaders to request her release. How he agreed to leave his *Englischer* lifestyle behind, make a kneeling confession, and rejoin the Amish—all in order to marry her! What love he must have in his heart to give up so much, for the little she had to offer.

She couldn't help the tears from pouring over onto her cheeks. Surely, they'd stain her apron but no matter. Elam loved her!

TWENTY-SEVEN

*I*f anyone had ever claimed that making a kneeling confession was an easy thing to do, they'd been lying. Elam's palms had been sweating, it seemed, since waking up this morning. It had been difficult to think of little else.

His folks had expressed how pleased they were with his return, and that had brought some measure of comfort. Humbling yourself and admitting your wrongdoing in front of a congregation of friends and loved ones was no simple task, especially when you didn't truly believe you'd done anything wrong. But it had been necessary to move forward, so he had accepted this challenge and kept his focus on the goal—marrying Julianna.

Now that the meeting was over, he could breathe a little easier. Julianna's father had said he could begin courting her after he made a kneeling confession. It was over now and he planned to initiate that courtship tonight.

He wanted to meet with Julianna's folks and discuss a

treatment plan for her. Would they be willing to work with him and go along with his desires concerning her health? He didn't know, but he would do his best to persuade them.

He'd already spoken with Zach on the matter and he'd offered some helpful suggestions. Elam planned to discuss that this evening.

Since they weren't married yet, Elam would need Julianna's father's permission to take her to see a health care practitioner. The sooner they began treatment, the better.

Elam sat at the kitchen table across from Obadiah Yoder, and glanced at Julianna who sat with her mother and siblings in the main gathering room. He'd wanted to discuss some of his hopes for Julianna's health without bringing distress to Julie, and felt the best way was to speak with her father alone. "Do you have a list of Julianna's medications?"

Her father nodded and went to a roll top desk that sat in the living room. He pulled open a drawer and brought out a small stack of papers. He handed them to Elam.

"Have you read over these?" Elam thumbed through them, examining the names of each one.

"*Nee.* Not so much. But the doctor said it was very important that she keep taking them." Obadiah sighed.

"Yes." Elam's eyes continued to scan the documents. "Did they inform you of the side effects?"

He shook his head.

"Says here that this drug could cause heart attack, stroke, thoughts of suicide…" Elam stopped reading. He lowered his tone. "These are really bad side effects. Why would they even have her on these?"

Obadiah shrugged. "Don't know."

"How has she been since she's been home? Has anything happened that has caused you to worry?" Because Elam was definitely starting to worry.

"She's just been quiet for the most part. Doesn't do much and we don't want to push her to do too much. She gets exhausted easily."

"I'd like to take her to a natural health doctor this week, if it's okay with you. You or your wife are welcome to come along. I'll pay for the driver and the appointment."

"That will be fine by me."

Elam wondered if perhaps physical therapy could benefit Julianna as well. That would be something to discuss with the doctor.

He glanced toward the living room. "Do you think she'd be up for a walk or a buggy ride?"

"You may ask her if you'd like. But don't keep her out too long. I don't know if she could handle it."

"I won't let anything happen to her." He stood, but Obadiah stopped him from leaving the table.

"Elam, I want to thank you for what you're doing for my *dochder*. I apologize for keeping her from you in the past. I didn't think that you two would make a good match, but I see now that I was wrong. You are good for her."

Elam had never been one for harboring bitterness, but

Obadiah Yoder's confession somehow brought vindication. "Thank you for saying that. I've only ever had Julianna's best interests in mind. Although I can't say I've always handled everything wisely."

"Who does?" Obadiah chuckled. "Shall we join the others?"

"*Jah.*" He held up the papers. "Do you mind if I take these home tonight and read them over?"

"No, do as you'd like."

"*Denki.*" He tucked them under his arm.

Julianna declined Elam's offer to go for a walk but agreed to a buggy ride. She'd been dying to get away from the house—from the watchful eye of *Mamm* and *Daed*. Since she'd been back, they'd treated her like one of the *kinner*.

"Are you glad to be back home?" Elam's magnetic blue eyes had always drawn her in. She'd imagined that gazing into their depths was like looking into the sea.

She watched Elam as he quietly guided the buggy along the country road and drank in the sight of the man who had rescued her. Her knight in shining armor. He was just as handsome as she remembered. No, even more so.

When they'd courted, she'd thought he was well built. He'd always been a hard worker and his frame evidenced that fact. But she could see that the areas that had been lacking as a youth were nicely filled in now. He was strong and solid. She'd felt that when his arms embraced her for the first time in the hospital.

She was still having a hard time believing that he'd asked to marry her. Why would he leave his *Englisch* lifestyle to take her as a wife? What did she have to offer?

Nothing. You have nothing to offer. He doesn't really love you. Look at yourself. You're ugly. You're fat. You're lazy. You will not make a good wife for him. You have nothing to offer.

"I have nothing to offer," she said.

Elam glanced at her and frowned. He reached over and lightly caressed her cheek. A slight smile lifted at the edge of his mouth. "I disagree."

Tell him to stop. Stop touching you.

"But I like it," she said.

"You like what?"

"You touching me."

His brow lifted. "Oh?"

She nodded liberally.

"What else do you like?"

Don't listen to him. Don't tell him.

She put her hands over her ears. "Be quiet. I want to listen."

"Julie, do you have voices inside your head?"

Voices.

She nodded.

"What are the voices telling you?"

She shrugged.

Elam smiled and scooted closer to her. He put one arm around her while the other one held the reins.

She liked that. She liked being close to Elam. She felt safe with him, protected.

"It's a nice evening, don't you think?" His gentle, yet masculine, voice set her at ease and relaxed her somehow.

She just wanted to snuggle in his arms—to stay there forever. "I don't want you to go."

"I will stay as long as I can tonight. But we can't live together yet. That will have to wait until we're married. We must abide by the *Ordnung*." He rubbed her shoulder. "I'll need to live at my folks' home until then. There are many things that will have to be done before we can marry. I'll be looking for a place for us to live in after we're married. Would you like to come along when I do that?"

"I don't like the *Ordnung*."

He chuckled. "I admit that there are parts of the *Ordnung* I don't like either. But they are the ways of our people and we must do our best to follow them." He looked at her. "So, was that a yes? Do you want to come along when I look at houses?"

"*Jah*."

"We're going to see a doctor this week. They are going to help you get better."

She shook her head. "I don't want medicine. I don't like

it."

"Well, this is a different kind of doctor that gives different kinds of medicines—natural ones. I plan to talk to them about the medicines that you're taking now. They are going to help you get better."

"Will they stop the voices?"

"I hope so."

"Me, too." She leaned over and put her head on Elam's chest. She heard his steady heartbeat through his shirt. It was a heartbeat she wished she could hear every day. This was her happy place, her favorite place. Next to Elam.

Elam looked at the clock on the wall. Two-thirty. Julie lay nestled in his arms on the couch in her folks' living room. But he didn't want to leave her. She clearly needed him.

He should probably get home, though. Morning milking would be in less than two hours and he'd still have to drive his rig home. He'd be lucky if he got any sleep at all.

He eased himself from the sofa, doing his best not to awaken her.

"Elam?"

"I need to go, *Schatzi*. And you should go get in your bed."

"Okay."

Elam released a relieved breath. He'd thought for sure

she'd put up a protest. He helped her from the couch and put his arm around her. "I'll walk you to your room."

She nodded.

"You'll have to tell me where it is." He smiled.

She pointed up.

"Upstairs? Okay." He released her from his embrace and gestured to the railing so she'd have something stable to hold onto. "I'll follow you."

She opened the door to her bedroom and he briefly wondered whether it was wise to enter. He decided against it.

She turned and he reached for her hand and pulled her close to him. He cupped the back of her head and brought his lips to hers. Her response delighted and surprised him.

"Goodnight, Julie."

TWENTY-EIGHT

*A*fter Elam dropped Julianna off for the evening, he thought of the night they'd 'officially' broken up. It was a place he hadn't visited often, because it had been too painful. But now that the world was right-side up again, he gave himself permission to think about the past.

It had been just like any other Sunday night, and he'd approached her after the singing. There she stood just as beautiful as ever.

"Are you ready to go, Julie?"

She frowned. "No, Elam. I…" She'd stopped midsentence and he followed her gaze. He turned to see what she'd been looking at.

Cletus Stolzfoos approached. "The rig's all hitched up, Julianna. Let's go?"

Julianna's eyes momentarily flitted to Elam's, then she nodded to Cletus. "*Jah*, I'm ready."

Elam's heart sank down into his stomach, it felt, as he watched Julianna pass him by and walk straight out of the house with Cletus. She didn't look back. Not even once.

He'd been too stunned to say anything, to do anything. There had been no explanation, no anything.

After she'd left with Cletus again at the next singing, Elam never returned. It hurt too much.

That was when he'd decided to leave the community, but not without first giving Julianna a piece of his mind. He'd headed out to the Yoder residence and found Julianna inside preparing supper. Fortunately, he hadn't seen her father around anywhere.

"Can you have someone else look after that? We need to talk." Elam did his best to keep his cool, as he stood near the back door. He didn't bother to remove his hat.

Julianna sighed, as though he'd ruined her day by showing up. "Uh, *jah*." She left the cook stove and beckoned one of her sisters, then met Elam outside.

"Do you want to walk?" He did his best to keep his wits about him. Not an easy task when he was close enough to take her in his arms and kiss her breathless.

She shrugged. "We can walk along the fence."

He stepped beside her. "I'm leaving."

She nodded but said nothing, just kept her gaze straight.

Fire burned in his veins and clenched his heart. "You don't even care, do you? Fine. You want to know something? I never cared for you either. At one time, I thought that maybe we had something special. But I was wrong. That's obvious.

"How can you just hook up with Cletus like that? Oh, *jah*, that's right. I forgot. He's rich. Well, fine. I can find me a girl who ain't a money grubber. One who's kind and smart and pretty. One day, I'll find a girl worthy of my love.

"You go ahead and court Cletus, but don't come looking for me if it don't work out. Because I won't be here."

He didn't even bother to look her way before stomping off. Perhaps she was shedding tears, he didn't know, but he didn't want to see it. And if she wasn't shedding tears, well, he didn't want to see that either. All he wanted to do was get away where he wouldn't have to think about or see Julianna with someone else.

How many times had he imagined himself and Julianna surrounded by loved ones while they took their vows? How many times had he dreamed of falling asleep with her in his arms? How many times had he looked forward to a houseful of *kinner* that mirrored the both of them?

The words he'd uttered had been nothing more than a boldfaced lie. Because, in truth, he had loved her with all his soul. In truth, if she had asked, he would have taken her back in a heartbeat. In truth, his heart had been on the verge of a complete meltdown.

"Ah, I see you're just in time for the morning milking." *Daed's* voice called from inside one of the barn stalls.

Elam groaned and placed the horse's tack he'd just removed onto its proper hook on the wall. He yawned. "Yep, I'm here."

"Perhaps next time you'll learn to come home a little earlier. I understand spending time with your *aldi*, but you need to consider other things as well, *Sohn*."

"It's been a long time since Julianna and I have been courting."

"*Jah*, but you will not make up for lost time in one night." His father turned and handed him two of the metal milk pails. "How did it go with her?"

"Well, Julie's quite a bit different from the last time we courted. She has changed much." Elam frowned, remembering the references she'd made to the voices.

"Spending that much time in a mental hospital is likely to change a body, I suppose." His father turned and looked him straight in the eye. "Marriage is a big commitment, *Sohn*. You know, no one would fault you if you decided not to marry her. If her problems are too burdensome—"

Elam stared back at him in utter revulsion. "Of course, I'm going to marry her. I promised her I would. I love her. I want to help her."

"I'm sorry. I didn't mean…"

"*Daed*, Julie needs me. If I won't help her, who will? If I won't protect her, who will? If I won't love her, then please tell me, who will?" Elam frowned. "Julianna is not a burden to bear, she is a blessing. I will care for her. I will cherish her. And with all that is in me, I will love her."

"I'm sure you will, Elam. But it won't be an easy road. You are going to need *Der Herr's* strength."

"I'm not looking for easy."

His father placed a hand on his forearm. "Your family will be here if you need us, *Sohn*."

"*Denki, Daed.*"

Elam wanted to be the person Julianna needed, longed to be what she needed, but doubts had begun surfacing. What if he wasn't good enough for her? What if he couldn't provide for all her needs? What if he failed as a husband?

Dear Gott, please help me. I cannot love her the way I should, the way she needs to be loved. Please place Your love in my heart so that I may love her as You would. Help me to see her and understand her through Your eyes, Lord. Amen.

TWENTY-NINE

*I*t seemed that life had been a flurry of activity since the moment Elam stepped back into the Amish community—from his kneeling confession, to Julianna's return home and courting her, his younger brother's wedding earlier this week, setting up Julianna's doctor's appointment, and having to sort through and dispose of all of his *Englisch* possessions. Elam longed for the quiet and simplicity his former *Englisch* life afforded. If folks thought things were easier or simpler in the Plain world, they were sorely mistaken. Of course, he supposed that the life of a single *Englischer* with few responsibilities couldn't be compared to an Amish man about to marry.

As he rode into town with a paid *Englisch* driver, Elam thought of his perfectly fine pickup truck sitting in his garage at his house in town. To have to pay someone for transportation just seemed ludicrous. He wished he could have just kept his own truck at his folks' house and used it until it was sold. But that wasn't the Amish way. And being under the watchful eye of the leadership until his proving was over, prevented him from doing many things he wished he could do.

As they neared his house, he noticed Zach's vehicle parked out in front.

"Thank you, Eric. Will you pick me up tomorrow at the same time? I should be ready by then." Elam stepped out of the car.

"Sure," Eric agreed before driving off.

The sight of seeing his former home both delighted and saddened him. Although he'd had good times here, he'd been lonely most of the time. Now, he had Julianna back in his life. And that was the part that made all this worthwhile.

"You ready to pack up this stuff?" Zach smiled.

"Ready as I'll ever be, I guess." Elam opened the garage and stared at his home gym with slight remorse. He'd miss that thing. "Hey, would you mind keeping this for me until Julianna and I move into our own place?"

Zach grinned. "You really think the leaders will approve of a home gym?"

"Probably not, but it's worth a try." The more he thought about keeping the gym, the more the idea grew on him. It would be a good activity for him and Julianna to participate in together. If the leaders insisted on him getting rid of it, he could always just give it to Zach and Rosanna or sell it.

"When is the realtor coming?"

"Tomorrow at two. I need to have everything out and the place cleaned up by then."

"That shouldn't be a problem, right?"

"Nope. Hey, thanks for agreeing to drive my truck to my folks' place and dropping off my stuff. I hate that it will have to sit in my folks' barn until I find a house, but at least Julie and I will have some furniture when we do move into our own place."

"Are you going to leave all your appliances?"

"Unless you want them or know of anyone who needs them. The realtor said that it's usually easier to sell a place like this if the appliances are left. Typically, first time home buyers are starting out with nothing."

Zach nodded. "Well, that's less stuff we have to move, right?"

"Right." Elam walked into the living room.

Zach lifted a stack of boxes. "How's everything going so far?"

"With Julie?"

Zach nodded and Elam followed him out to the pickup.

"Pretty well, I think. I already knew we'd have to deal with issues. But I am concerned about the medications the doctors have her on. I read over the side effects the other day." He shook his head and slid the boxes into the back of the truck bed. "I wish she didn't have to take them."

"Maybe she doesn't."

"What do you mean?" They walked back into the house.

"I've heard that doctors can tend to be a little overzealous when it comes to prescribing medications. It might be great for their wallets but it's not always so great for their patients. I believe I read that psychiatric prescription over usage is one of the worst. They label normal human emotions as diseases then prescribe medicine for those diseases. Come to think of it, there was some big documentary on it that I watch one time. You should watch it." Zach and Elam carefully placed the bureau onto the truck. "Do you know why she is on them and what each one was prescribed for?"

"The papers say what they are for. Maybe she does need some of them. I just don't see why she has to take so many. It's not good. She says she has voices in her head."

"If I were you, I'd figure out if she needs them and what she needs them for. There are other types of therapy other than medication. I know many of the folks with PTSD that come out to our horse ranch have been able to discontinue their medication." Zach lifted one end of the futon as Elam did the same with the other side. "If you think about it, most people take medication because something is wrong. But it wasn't the lack of medication that made things wrong in the first place. The medication is only covering the symptoms, it's not addressing them. If you could find out how to address her problems directly and help her heal from whatever is going on inside her, then she won't need the medicine."

Elam set his end of the couch on the truck's bed and they both slid it in. "Do you think the horses could help Julie too?"

"Sure, animals are great therapy. Anything positive that can get her mind off herself and her troubles will be beneficial. I bet Scramble can help too."

Elam thought about his dog out at his folks' place. He'd adjusted better than Elam had thought he would. He never lacked for attention with Elam's siblings around. Hopefully, he'd be just as content when Elam and Julianna got their own home. "*Jah*, he loves the farm."

After Elam and Zach had emptied out the house and dropped off his belongings at his parents' place, they returned to Zach and Rosanna's for supper and the remainder of the evening. Tomorrow, Elam would return to his house one last time to give it a thorough cleaning, then he would go back to his folks' home until he found a piece of property for himself and Julianna.

Elam had already talked to a realtor about helping him find a house in the area. The realtor had said that there were a couple of properties that might be of interest to him within their Amish district, however, both were *Englisch* homes and would require removal of the electric. Elam wished he could keep it.

THIRTY

For some reason, Elam hadn't expected the naturopathic doctor to be a woman. But perhaps a female would be best for Julie.

After he gave the doctor the rundown of Julianna's condition, she seemed to have a keen understanding of the situation as though she'd dealt with it many times in the past. Elam hoped that was true, because he desired nothing more than to see Julie happy and well.

Julianna was in another room with the therapist, while the doctor reviewed the natural healing protocol with Elam. At first, he'd worried about Julie being separated from him but the therapist quickly put him at ease when she struck up a casual conversation with Julianna. Julie willingly stayed in the other room with the therapist and showed no signs of anxiety.

"What I suggest is a total wellness approach that encompasses body, soul, and spirit.

"For the body—and this is one of the most important keys—is diet. She needs to avoid junk food, sugars, and animal products as much as possible."

Elam blinked. "Animal products?"

"Yes. Meat, dairy, eggs. Anything that comes from an animal. I realize this part is difficult for most people to understand since it's been ingrained in us since birth practically. But independent research has shown that animal proteins play a key factor in most diseases—like cancer."

Elam frowned. This is what they lived on mostly—fresh eggs from the chickens and milk and cheese from their cows. "What will she eat, then?"

The way she smiled at him made him feel like he was ten years old, but he didn't consider it an insult. "There is an abundance of food in the plant kingdom, chock full of the vitamins and minerals our bodies need and crave."

"You want her to eat plants?"

"Things that grow from the soil. The things mother nature has provided for us."

God provided for us, Elam mentally corrected.

"Fruits, vegetables, nuts, seeds, non-GMO whole grains. There are plenty of non-animal foods available for our consumption. I also recommend a daily juicing regimen."

"Juicing?"

"Do you own a juicer?"

He wasn't even sure what a juicer was. "No."

"That will need to be your first purchase. As soon as you leave here, before you go home, you should stop by the store and pick up a juicer."

"Does this juicer work on electric?"

"Electricity? Yes."

"Our district does not allow electric of any kind."

"Not even for health reasons? I would think they would make an exception for that. I can come and discuss it with the leaders if it will help. Owning and using a juicer is imperative for good health."

"How will she get her protein if she doesn't eat animal products?"

She smiled. "The Amish read the Bible, right?"

"Yes." He wondered what this had to do with their conversation, but allowed her to continue.

"Do you know what God told Adam and Eve to eat—what their bodies were designed for?"

Elam shook his head.

"Plants, fruits, seeds—all things that come directly from the earth. Which, if you think about it, makes a lot of sense. If God made them from the dust of the earth, then it's what comes from that very soil which will nourish them properly. As far as I know, God never redesigned the human body." She handed him a booklet. "Also, if you think about some of the largest creatures in the animal kingdom—the gorilla, the bear, the horse, the elephant—they all exist primarily on plant foods. If plants contain enough protein for those massive creatures—and they are *really* strong—don't you think plants are sufficient for humans as well?"

He scratched his head. "Hmm...never thought of that

before. But you're right, it does make a lot of sense."

"Now, with this regimen, she's probably going to feel sick at times. Especially in the first week. But don't be alarmed, this is completely normal and necessary."

"But I thought these things were supposed to help her."

"And they will. What will be happening inside Julianna is basically like a housecleaning for the body. The food and herbs will gather the toxins and remove them. After this detoxification takes place, her body will be able to assimilate the nutrients contained in the food much more readily. Before you know it, she will feel great."

Elam blew out a breath and nodded. This wasn't going to be an easy thing, it seemed. But he had told his father that he wasn't looking for easy.

"Next, we will start with a light exercise regimen. As she improves and gains more energy, we'll gradually increase the physical activity. The more she is outside amongst nature and exposed to natural sunlight, the better. Sunshine and fresh air can be wonderful healers."

Elam nodded, attempting to keep a mental list in his head.

"For the soul, which encompasses the mind, will, and emotions, I recommend things that will stimulate her mind in a positive manner. The key here is to disallow any negative thought process. Have you ever heard that laughter is the best medicine?"

"*Jah.*" Elam thought of the verse from the Bible, *A merry heart doeth good like a medicine.*

"I usually recommend that patients watch comedic videos, but in this case, we'll have to think outside the box." She tapped a finger on her chin. "Have you heard of Zig Ziglar?"

"No."

"I suggest going to your local library and requesting his audiobooks. They should have comedians' CDs too, now that I think about it. Some Christian entertainers include Mark Lowry, Tim Hawkins, Chonda Pierce, Thor Ramsey, Ken Davis, Michael Junior." She smiled. "You can tell I recommend them a lot, can't you? I can write out a list for you. Just make a request to the librarian and she should get them for you. They will be good for both of you to listen to. Or do you not have a way to listen to CDs?" Her lips twisted.

"We can figure something out." He thought of the portable CD player he sometimes used when he went on walks.

"Another thing I would suggest is helping or doing things for others. This could include making meals, giving gifts, giving of your time—anything to take the focus off oneself and to consider others' needs.

"As far as the spiritual side goes, I realize the Amish are deeply spiritual people. At least this is what I have heard, am I correct?"

Elam wasn't sure how to answer that question. Sure, their people attended meeting every other week, prayed before meals, had dutiful Bible readings, but to say they were deeply spiritual didn't sit well in his mind. They were bound by the rules and mandates of the church, more of an outward obedience than the inner peace that comes from knowing Christ and walking with Him daily.

"We attend meeting," he simply said.

"That's good. Whatever spiritual activities you participate in, I encourage you to continue in those things."

Elam thought that it would be wonderful to bring Julianna to the *Englisch* church he'd attended with Zach. Surely, she'd get much more out of the service than the methodical practices of their Amish meetings. Now that he thought about it, attending meeting, with its somberness, could potentially have a negative effect on Julianna. But they couldn't not attend, that was a non-negotiable.

"Okay, here is all the paperwork you need including everything I just told you as well as instructions. If you want Julianna to get well, it is imperative that you follow this regimen. Call me at any time if you have any questions or concerns. If something's not working, we can tweak the program for her."

He looked over the papers. "What is a rebounder?"

"It's a piece of exercise equipment, it looks very similar to a mini-trampoline, but it has more springs and they're quite a bit stronger. You can find them online." She frowned. "Oh, I keep forgetting. You don't use computers, do you?"

"I can have a friend look it up for me."

She nodded in satisfaction. "Good idea. Any other questions or concerns?"

"What about her medications? Should she stop taking those?"

"Oh, by all means, no."

"No?" His brow lowered. That was one of the main reasons they were here, to get Julianna off her medication. "But she talks about voices inside her head."

The doctor nodded. "Hearing voices is a typical side effect of psychotropic medication. I've heard many clients claim this. As a matter of fact, many of the mass shootings that have happened in recent years were perpetrated by people under the influence of these drugs.

"However, we must weigh the risks and benefits and consider the consequences all around. Taking her off those medications cold turkey could kill her. We will measure her progress to see where she is at and how she is coping *after* thirty days of the protocol I've detailed in those papers. If I feel she is adjusting well, we might begin to gradually taper off her medication. The only safe way is to slowly adjust her meds, and even then, she will probably experience some withdrawal or detoxification symptoms."

Elam didn't know if he liked the sound of that, but he would listen to this doctor. She seemed to know a lot more about these things than he did.

"It could take a year or maybe even longer, but I am confident it will be worth it," she assured, then glanced down at her clipboard. The doctor held up her index finger. "Another thing…are you and your fiancée currently using any kind of birth control?"

Heat immediately crept up his neck at the insinuation. How was this anybody's business? He was glad that Julianna wasn't present to hear these words.

Elam shook his head. "We haven't...we are not married yet."

"Well, that's refreshing to hear. You never know nowadays. It would probably be best to wait to have children until Julianna is off her medication and her body has completely detoxified from it. Conceiving at this point in time could be detrimental to the baby and cause serious complications."

Elam frowned. He'd never considered this aspect. He'd hoped to have a child when God chose to bless them with one. For most married couples, that happened in the first year of marriage. "You said it will take over a year for Julie to be off her medication?"

"That's correct. I can suggest some natural birth control methods if you'd like."

"Our people believe in trusting God's timing for children."

"You can still trust God's timing. What I'm referring to is simply abstaining during certain days of the month. I think this would be wise." She turned and added a couple of papers to the others. "I'll just leave these with you so you can look them over and pray about it."

Elam nodded. "Thank you very much, doctor."

Elam sighed as he and Julianna headed back home. There were so many things to consider. How different their lives would be in comparison with other newly married couples. Their path was truly an uphill battle, but the doctor had seemed positive that Julianna could heal and they could have a normal life together. And *that* was encouraging.

"Eric, we'll need to go by Walmart before we go home. Do you mind? We shouldn't be too long."

"No problem, Elam," the driver responded.

A few moments later, their driver dropped them off in front of the store and parked the vehicle. He'd said he'd stay in the car and wait.

"Do you know what a juicer is?" Elam asked Julianna as they headed toward the appliance section of the store.

She shook her head.

He quickly found the aisle and chose the machine that looked the sturdiest. "See." He showed her the picture on the back of the box. "You put vegetables and fruit inside that chute and juice comes out into the glass. Pretty cool, huh?"

Julianna smiled and he grasped her hand. He led the way to the entertainment section of the store and Elam picked up some extra batteries and a set of small speakers to use with his CD player. He thought that listening to the comedy CDs from the library would be a good activity while they were out riding around in his buggy, whether courting or going to look at houses to buy. They finally approached the register and he paid for the items.

Now, he just needed to pray that the leaders would allow them to use the electric juicer. It was true that they didn't have electricity hooked up to their houses, but they did occasionally use generators that ran on gasoline and could power an electrical appliance if need be. He wondered if it would be wiser to just use the appliance and not say anything or go to the leaders and ask for permission first.

Since he was still going through his time of proving, he decided the best thing to do was let Obadiah Yoder handle the matter. After all, Julianna would be living under their roof for several more weeks until Elam and Julianna married. A day Elam looked forward to more with each passing moment.

THIRTY-ONE

"*E*lam, Deacon Schwartz is here to see you." His father stood near the door and called him from the supper table.

Oh no. A visit from the deacon usually did not include glad tidings of great joy.

"Yes?" Elam approached. "Would you like to take a seat, Deacon?"

"*Nee.* Is it true that you have brought the *Englisch* ways to our people?"

Elam frowned. "*Englisch* ways? I'm not sure I know what you mean."

"Did you not purchase an appliance that runs on electric?" The deacon clarified.

"Oh, you mean the juicer I bought for Julianna?"

"*Jah.* You know it is *verboten.* Why would you bring it into this community?"

"Julianna needs it for her health. The doctor insisted on it." He hoped that didn't mean Julianna's family hadn't been using it. The sooner her health was restored, the better it would be for everyone.

"And the doctor's words hold more meaning to you than the *Ordnung*?"

Elam clenched his hands at his side in frustration. "Are you telling me that Julianna has to stay sick because the leaders won't approve of the juicer?"

"We do not approve of the use of electric. You *are* aware of this." The deacon's stance was firm.

"How, then, do you expect her to get well if she can't use the tools needed to get her well? As far as I know, there are no juicers that run on propane. Besides, some of the men in the community use a generator for their tools."

"That is different. It is for their livelihood and to provide for their own."

Elam did his best not to blow his top, but he found it extremely difficult. "And you're saying that Julianna's *life* is not important enough to make an exception?"

This was one thing that bothered him about his community. Their decisions were hypocritical at times. These rules made absolutely no sense.

Deacon Schwartz remained silent.

"Can I have a meeting with the leaders?" Elam frowned.

"This situation has already been discussed. That is why I am here."

"What do you want me to do?"

"Return the juicer to the store."

Elam stood open-mouthed. If he said something, it could possibly cause him to have more proving time—if he didn't already. If he kept quiet and agreed, he could marry Julianna as quickly as possible and leave the community if that was what it would take to get her well.

"I will do as you say." He forfeited – for now.

"*Gut.*" Deacon Schwartz nodded. "I knew you would see that our ways are best. You are a wise man, Elam."

Elam kept his cool as he watched the deacon leave his folks' property. But what he felt like doing was running off with Julianna tonight, marrying her, and living *Englisch* for at least as long as it took to get her better. But what if she needed a special diet and lifestyle for the rest of her life? Would they stay separated from their families for as long as they lived? Somehow, he knew that would not be healthy for Julianna either. It didn't matter what he did—either way, they'd lose.

Elam had thought of the idea last night, but it had been too late to call Zach. Now, as he walked toward the phone shanty, a spark of hope kindled in his soul. What if they did sell juicers that ran on propane or some other non-electric source? Surely there had been others with a similar dilemma.

He quickly dialed Zach's phone number.

"Hello?"

"Hey, Zach, it's Elam. Do you know if there is such a

thing as a vegetable juicer that runs on propane?"

"I have no idea, man. Just a sec and I'll look it up online."

Elam heard the sound of keys typing on a keyboard.

"Uh, okay. No, I don't see anything on a propane juicer. Sorry."

Elam felt like someone had taken a needle and stuck it into his balloon of hope.

"Wait. It looks like they have some type of manual juicer. It's plastic. It doesn't look the sturdiest, but it might work. Do you want me to go ahead and order it? It looks like it's about thirty bucks."

"*Jah*, sure. Please, if you will."

"No problem. Hey, how's everything going?"

"It's frustrating, but I'm trying my best not to do anything to lengthen my proving time."

"I hear you."

"Have you and Rosanna been back to Honey Ridge lately?"

"Not lately. It's really hard going back. I have so many memories there. I miss John so much, I can only imagine how Rosanna feels. I'm sure it's worse for her. And then there are our families constantly trying to get us to come back, warning of Hell. I'm sure you know all about it."

"*Jah*, I definitely get it. It's extra hard when you know what both worlds are like. Each one has its own appeal."

"Isn't that the truth?"

"Well, I'll let you go. I'm sure you have many things to do, as do I."

"Okay. I'll let you know when that juicer comes in. It says about a week and a half."

"*Gut*. That's not too bad." He didn't want to wait at all when it came to Julianna's health, but he had to take what he could get.

THIRTY-TWO

$\mathcal{S}$undays always brought a smile to Elam's lips—especially the non-church Sundays when they could spend the day visiting with family or friends.

Today, that meant picking up Julie in his buggy and bringing her home to share a meal with his family. It also meant he'd be seeing Danny and his new wife for the first time since their wedding. Elam had wanted to visit with him sooner, but he had no desire to go near the Stolzfoos ranch.

This coming week, he planned to spend most of the time in town working with Merlin Yost, a conservative Mennonite man who'd hired Elam before he'd left the Amish. Elam was grateful for his shed-building job. It provided enough money to live on and to give a little extra to his folks. But since he'd be taking on a new bride soon, he'd probably need a little more, especially if he had to provide for Julianna's medication, doctor visits, and whatever else she'd need.

He'd asked *Mamm* earlier in the week to be sure to have non-animal foods available for Julianna to eat. At first, his mother wasn't sure what she could make that would be acceptable for Julie, but when she returned home from the store with a smile on her face, Elam knew she'd succeeded in finding suitable nourishment. He planned to eat the same foods Julianna ate so she wouldn't feel awkward while the others ate different foods.

Elam tugged on the reins, bringing his driving horse to a halt. He tethered the reins to the hitching post and stepped onto the porch of Julie's folks' home. He knocked, and was surprised when Julianna opened the door.

"Hi." Her timid smile endeared her to him even more.

"Hi." He smiled back, longing to bring her close and kiss her lips. He looked over her shoulder and noticed her mother standing in the kitchen, then fixed his eyes on her again. "You ready to go?"

"*Jah.*" Julianna reached for his hand, surprising him once again.

They stepped up into the buggy. "You look well. How are you feeling?"

"*Gut.*"

"How is your health regimen going?"

She grimaced a bit. "It's getting better. I was sick the first week."

"The doctor said most people get sick the first week." Elam nodded. "But you feel better now?"

"*Jah.* Mostly."

"I can tell. You look better. Healthier." Elam grinned.

"How is the manual juicer working out? Is it good enough?"

She shrugged. "*Mamm* doesn't care much for it."

"But it does the job, right? I'm going to see if I can figure out how to convert an electric juicer. I think that will be easier than trying to convince the elders to allow us to use electricity."

She snuggled close to his side and he draped his arm around her shoulders, pulling her as near as space would allow. He couldn't wait until they had their own place and they could snuggle as much as they wanted to. He kissed the top of her head.

"My *mamm* is making some *gut* food for us. Beans and rice, I think, and green salad."

"*Ach*, that sounds *wunderbaar*." She reached into her purse and pulled out an apple, a banana, and a container of juice. "I brought these just in case."

"Is that carrot juice?"

"*Jah, Mamm* made a little while ago."

"May I taste it? I've never tried carrot juice before."

"It's very *gut*. I like it."

Elam's brow shot up. "You do?"

She nodded and handed Elam the container without the lid.

He took a drink, not knowing what to expect. "Mm...this is really *gut*. It's sweet."

"*Jah*."

Elam exhaled a sigh of relief. For some reason, he'd

expected a strict, healthy diet to be devoid of taste—or taste terrible. But so far, he'd learned that most of the things Julianna consumed had been very flavorful and satisfying to the taste buds.

He handed the plastic container back to her.

"You may drink more."

He shook his head. "I'd love to. But your *mudder* did not go to all that trouble to make that drink for me." He squeezed her hand. "Guess what? I've got good news."

"You found a house?"

He couldn't mask his grin. "Maybe. Remember the little house on ten acres that I was telling you about? We can look at it tomorrow when I get off work."

Julianna squealed and squeezed his arm.

He looked at her in amazement. "You really are doing better. This is the best I've seen you since you've come home. I like it." He smiled and clasped her chin. "You're cute, you know that?"

She shook her head.

"Are you insulting my intelligence?" He crossed his arms in mock offense.

Julie grinned.

"Can you believe it? Two more weeks." With each day that passed, he looked forward to making Julianna his wife. "*Daed* said we're free to use the *dawdi haus* until we find a place of our own. I've already moved some of the furniture in."

"Really? May I see it today?"

The excitement in her voice brought a thrill to his soul. He loved seeing this side of Julie. It reminded him of what they used to have, and what could be. "You bet."

He maneuvered the horse to the hitching post and tethered her until he'd made quick work of unhitching the buggy. Scramble met him and Julianna as they headed toward the house. Elam crouched down and rubbed the dog's head, scratching behind his ears the way he liked it. "Hey, Scramble. You remember Julie?"

Scramble wagged his tail as Julie pet him as well. "You're a good boy," she said.

Elam recognized the enjoyment of the mutual relationship between Julianna and Scramble. Indeed, his canine companion would serve her well. Elam was glad that Scramble would be present to keep company with Julie while he was away at work during the week. Truth be told, that was something that had him worried. He didn't want to leave her alone, didn't know how it would affect her emotionally. Perhaps they should get a cat for inside the house as well.

THIRTY-THREE

Elam couldn't believe this day was finally here—the day he and Julianna would become husband and wife. It was a day he had hoped for, fantasized about, prayed for, and dreamed about many times in the past. A dream that had died. A dream that had been buried. A dream that had been resurrected. A dream that was now a reality. *Denki, Gott.*

It seemed like every rule and tradition in their Amish church district had been compromised in the weeks immediately following Julianna's release from the hospital. The leaders agreed to allow her to take classes for baptism *after* they married, something that had been unheard of as far as Elam knew, reasoning that Elam had already been baptized and had made a kneeling confession. Elam had also reasoned with them that Julianna's medication would probably impair her ability to memorize the parts of the *Dortrecht Confession of Faith* that would be required of her. With that being the case, they married within six weeks of her release—just after his proving time was over.

It felt like God had given him a second chance—it was a miracle, indeed.

As they stood in front of the leaders and their community of family and friends in Julianna's neighbors' home, Elam's heart soared. He glanced down at his and Julianna's clasped hands. The look of love in her sparkling hazel-green eyes embedded itself somewhere deep inside his chest. Oh, how he loved to see her happy.

Elam knew they had a difficult road ahead of them. He knew that not every day would be sunshine and roses, but it didn't matter. Because he also knew that *Der Herr* would see them through whatever obstacles came their way. The joy of the Lord would be his strength. He just needed to remember that when the difficult days presented themselves.

Just then, Elam reminded himself of something his *grossmammi* in Ohio used to say. *When the going gets tough, the tough get praying. Jah*, he'd need to remember that.

Their wedding day had been full of fun and games, and special memories had been made. But as the night wore on, Elam sensed that Julie was exhausted. Perhaps they should have left sooner.

Tonight they'd spend the night at Julie's folks' place and help with the cleanup at the neighbors' place tomorrow, then they'd move into the *dawdi haus* on his folks' property. Elam looked forward to some peace and quiet and time alone with his wife.

Today was definitely the beginning of a new adventure.

Elam awakened to the sound of murmuring in the kitchen. He rolled over onto his side and allowed his gaze to roam over his wife while she slept.

Although she'd only been on her wellness regimen for about a month, he could already see the physical effects it was having on her.

Her skin appeared to have taken on a glow of sorts. The doctor had said not to be alarmed if her skin turned a yellowish-orange, and that this was a natural result of drinking the carrot juice and a sign that the body was doing its job in detoxifying itself.

Another thing he'd noticed was that her weight had decreased and she appeared to be slimmer than when he'd seen her in the psychiatric hospital. From the literature he'd read, he knew the weight gain was a common side effect of the medication she'd been taking.

But what he was most excited about was the effect it seemed to be having on her emotions. She seemed to have more and more good days and fewer bad days.

He leaned close and kissed her cheek, but did his best not to awaken her. No doubt she was tuckered out from the night before. By the time they'd reached home last night, Julianna had already fallen asleep on his shoulder. He had carefully lifted her from the buggy and deposited her where she still lay, peacefully sleeping in the blue hand-sewn dress she'd worn for their wedding ceremony.

He quickly dressed and went to the kitchen, where he'd heard activity earlier. Perhaps he could help with chores or begin cleaning up at the neighbor's house from last night's festivities.

"Would you like a cup of coffee, Elam?" Julianna's mother offered.

He rubbed the sleep from his eyes and yawned. "That would be *wunderbaar, denki.*"

"Julianna is still sleeping?"

"*Jah.* I wanted to let her rest. She was very tired last night." He took a sip of the steaming beverage in from of him, the heat scalding his taste buds. He never understood how some people could drink their coffee so hot.

She held up a mason jar with white liquid inside. "Would you like some milk?"

"Yes, please." She smiled and he poured some in, dropping the temperature down to something drinkable.

"She usually awakens about ten."

Elam's eyes widened. "Ten?"

"*Jah,* then I will make her carrot juice."

"I can make it for her today. Will you show me how you normally do it?"

Julie's mother smiled. "Sure."

He watched as she removed the plastic contraption from the cupboard and took the carrots he purchased every week from the ice box. The electric juicer the elders had rejected seemed much better suited for the task then the flimsy manual machine he now stared at.

Her mother proceeded to cut the carrots into smaller pieces, then fed them through the juicer's small chute using the hand crank to push them through to the masticator. Juice dripped into a plastic cup from the bottom and the pulp came out the side and dropped into a bowl.

"The goats love the pulp," she commented, then handed the cup of juice to him.

"That doesn't seem too bad." He drank the little bit of juice.

"*Nee*, but I tell you that the muscles in my arm have gotten stronger since I started juicing for my *dochder*." She chuckled. "Worst part is probably the cleanup. It takes a while to scrub all those little fibers out."

"And you do this three times a day?"

"*Jah*. I can tell it's helping her though." She stuck a finger in the air. "Which reminds me, did she take her medicines last night?"

"Oh, no. I didn't even think about it. She'd fallen asleep..." *Dummkopp*. How could he have forgotten?

"We forgot one time." She frowned. "She didn't do well."

"What do you mean?" Elam swallowed.

"She wasn't the same. She was angry, seemed withdrawn, kept saying strange things." Her mother sighed. "Why don't you stay here with her today and let us tend to the cleanup at the Borntregers'? I'm certain sure she'll do better with you."

"I can do that. But are you sure? I can go help out right now and then return at ten when she awakens." He'd feel much more useful doing something, especially since he wasn't in his own home.

"Whatever you'd like to do, Elam."

Several hours later, Elam wiped the sweat from his brow and set the broom on its hook in the utility room. He glanced around the Borntregers' gathering room and nodded in satisfaction. Now, he just needed to help move the furniture back into place. He looked up at the clock. Eight-thirty. He decided it was about time to go back to the Yoders' place to see if Julianna had awakened yet. He'd do that just as soon as the job here was complete.

Half an hour later, he stepped onto the porch of the Yoders' home but stopped before opening the door. He heard loud voices coming from inside. One of them sounded like Julianna's. He quickly opened the door.

"No! I don't want it!" Julianna screamed.

"You need to take it," her mother urged, holding out her pills.

Elam walked into the room just in time to see Julianna throw her medication across the room.

"Julie?" He glanced to her mother, then back to her and frowned. "What is this? What's going on?"

Her mother sighed in relief. "Oh, *gut*. You're here. She refuses to take her medicine."

Elam nodded and silently prayed for wisdom. "I'll handle it."

"*Denki*, Elam. I must go tend to the wash." Her mother excused herself, clearly frustrated.

Elam cautiously walked over to Julianna. He ignored the pills on the floor and stood in front of her. He reached up and caressed her face and brought her gaze to his. "*Schatzi*, come."

He silently led her back to the bedroom they'd slept in. He sat on the bed and patted the spot next to him. Julianna sat down in compliance.

He took her hands in his and bowed his head. He decided to pray aloud so Julie could hear the prayer as well. "Dear *Gott*, thank You for this beautiful day that You have made. Thank You for my wife, whom I love very much. Please be with us today in everything that we say and everything that we do. Let the words of our mouths and the meditation of our hearts be acceptable in Thy sight, oh, Lord. Give us the strength we need to honor You today. Amen."

Elam draped his arm around Julie's shoulder and pulled her close. "I love you, *Schatzi*."

Julianna broke down and began weeping. "*Nee.*"

"Yes, I do." He moved to stand in front of her and crouched down to her level. He cradled her face in his hands then took a handkerchief from his pocket and wiped away her tears. He placed a gentle kiss on her lips. "You are more special to me than anyone in the world. I want you to get better. I want you to be happy."

She nodded.

"Will you do me a favor and take your medicine? I will make you some juice to drink too."

"I like juice."

Elam smiled in relief. "Good. Me, too. I'll make some for both of us."

The remainder of the day had gone a little more smoothly, which Elam had thanked God for many times. He told himself that he would never again forget to give Julianna her medicine. He had to remind himself that this was not who Julie was. It was only a cycle in life's garden that they had to plow through in order to cultivate a harvest. Eventually. Until then, it would take time, patience, and a diligent purposeful tending to, in order to bring forth fruit.

THIRTY-FOUR

*E*lam wiped the final dish and placed it into the cupboard of his folks' *dawdi haus*, where they'd been staying. He whispered a silent prayer of thankfulness for the progress Julie had made. There were good days and bad days, it seemed.

This was a good day. She'd spoken much more than usual at supper tonight and she'd helped with the dishes. Since she seemed to be in a talkative mood, perhaps now would be a good time to get her to open up about the past.

"*Schatzi*, I'd like to talk to you about something. I want you to be honest. You don't need to fear me getting upset. But I'd like to understand some things." He rubbed her forearm. "Are you willing to open up to me?"

"I...I don't know."

He wanted to give her the reassurance she needed. He moved to sit in front of her and took her hands in his. "I promise that nothing that you've said or done in the past will make me love you less. And the same holds true now. You need not ever worry about that."

She nodded.

"I've heard rumors, but I want to hear the truth from you. Will you tell me why they sent you away?"

"It's a very long story."

"We're not going anywhere and I've got all night." He smiled. "Will you share your story with me, please?"

"It started after you left. Cletus Stolzfoos was courting me at the time." She looked into his eyes, her expression hesitant.

He nodded. "I asked. You may continue."

"We had been dating for a several months and things seemed to be getting more serious. One night, we were at home and just sitting and talking like usual." She squeezed her eyes shut for a moment. "He put his hand on me, under my dress, when we were kissing."

Elam felt like going over to Cletus' house right now and giving him a piece of his mind—and maybe something else. Instead, he did his best to keep his wits about him so Julianna would continue her story.

"I moved his hand away and told him no, that I didn't want him to do that. He tried to persuade me to go to my bedroom, said no one would know. He said that other people who were serious were doing that, and we'd probably be getting married before long." She shook her head. "But I refused. *You* set a good standard for me, I think. I told him that I would only do that after I was married."

"Good." Elam sighed in relief.

"He left right away. He was angry with me. He didn't say as much, but I could tell. That was the last time he took me home from a singing." She shrugged. "It didn't really bother me that much. I never loved him like…"

"Like?"

"Like you. You know it wasn't my choice to break things off with you. You know I had to obey my father. And so that is what I did, although I would have rather been with you."

"I wish you would have left with me."

"Looking back now, I wish I would have too."

"So, what happened after Cletus?"

"Well, he started a rumor, you see. He told everyone, or at least the boys in his gang, that we had…you know…and he said that I broke up with him because I wanted a different boy. One by one, those other boys asked me to ride home in their buggies. I had no idea Cletus had said anything. Anyway, after going with about three boys that all tried to get me to do something, one of them said something about me and Cletus. I told him the truth but he didn't believe me. After that, I just stopped going to singings all together.

"But somehow the word got out and everyone, including my father, believed the rumors to be true. It was terrible, Elam. I'd wished with all my heart that I'd gone with you to the *Englisch*. But the last time we talked, you'd said not to come looking for you. You'd told me that you never really cared." She chuckled. "I hadn't believed you back then when you'd said it, but somehow I talked myself into believing it at that time in my life. So I never went looking.

"It was a lot of pressure with everyone staring at me all the time and whispering. I didn't have any friends anymore—just my sister Naomi and my cousin Martha who had moved into the community. I told her that I just wanted to go and find you. I told her that I wanted to live with you in the *Englisch* world—far away from everyone talking about me. Martha was concerned, I think, and she told *Daed*. He went and talked to the elders about it all—the rumors, me talking about jumping the fence, and about me crying all the time. I thought my life was over. I thought I was destined to become and *alt maedel* and remain childless my whole life."

"And that was when they sent you away, right?"

She nodded.

"So, they thought it would solve all their problems. No one would be gossiping around you. The crying gave them a reason to deem you 'depressed' and have you committed. And you'd still be safely Amish, thus protecting your soul from Hell."

"I think a lot of folks probably thought I went away to have a baby. Only a few people knew where I really was."

"Julie, I was wrong to say those words. I only spoke them out of grief. I'm so sorry I wasn't here for you. I should have come back to check on you sooner, but I was sure you'd already gotten married and just the thought of it tore me up inside. I finally did come because I had to satisfy my curiosity, at least, that's what I'd thought. But now I know that it was God leading me to you all along."

"I'm so glad you came looking for me, Elam."

"It was God. God wants you to know His love, Julie. He wants to heal you and bring you peace. Will you let Him do that?"

"I don't know how."

"Jesus will come and live inside your heart if you ask Him to come in."

"Will He talk to me like the other voices?"

"I hope He will silence the other voices. And because you will be His sheep, you will know His voice—the voice of the Shepherd."

She looked hesitant and Elam wasn't sure how well she understood his explanation.

"If you would like to pray, I can help you."

She shrugged.

Elam sensed that she wasn't ready and he didn't want to encourage her to make a false profession. Instead, he chose to pray that God would open her eyes and draw her to Him. He really desired for Julie to get saved, but he also knew that God's timing was perfect.

THIRTY-FIVE

"How is Julianna doing with her decrease in meds?" The doctor examined the clipboard cradled in her arm.

"Pretty good, I think," Elam said, wondering how her current therapy session was going.

"Is she still having more good days than bad days?"

"*Jah.*"

"She will most likely continue to have issues here and there." The doctor peered over the clipboard. "Even after she has been completely weaned. Remember the withdrawal symptoms we talked about on her first visit?"

"Yes, but you said that those symptoms will eventually disappear."

"That's right. Do you still have the paper on coping skills?"

He attempted to remember which paper that was. "I think so."

"I want you to review that paper with her. It's important that she knows how to divert her thoughts when things get rough. Our phone number is on that paper along with the suicide hotline. Having someone to talk things through with can be the difference between life and death."

Elam swallowed and nodded. He hated to think that Julianna would loath herself and her life so much that she would attempt to end it. But as the doctor had reminded him, it wasn't her but the effects of the medication that brought on these harmful thoughts.

"Before we go shopping, I'd like to visit Zach's ranch. Do you mind?" Elam whispered to Julianna in the backseat of their driver's car.

"That's fine."

Elam informed their driver, then asked him to pick them up at the grocery store in a couple of hours. They'd have Zach drop them off at the store.

The driver pulled up to Zach's place and let them off. "I'll be at Walmart at three then."

"Sounds *gut*." Elam nodded and watched him drive off. He turned to Julianna. "*Kumm*."

They walked toward the barn and found Zachariah near a stall, surrounded by a few young men. The group turned as he and Julianna walked up.

"E? Is that you, bro?" One of the young men asked as he stared at Elam and Julianna. "What's with the threads, man?"

Elam chuckled. "I'm Amish now."

"I can see you got yourself a woman." Mischief sparkled in the young man's eyes.

"Not just any woman." Elam squeezed Julie's hand and grinned. "This is my wife."

The young man's mouth hung open. "You got yourself hitched too?"

"That's right. Meet Julianna."

The young men came near and patted him on the back. Some shook his hand and Julianna's hand.

"Julie, this is Tyrone, Paco, Mikey, JJ, and Homer," Elam introduced.

Julianna's expression was full of questions.

Elam explained. "They're good friends of mine. We've spent a lot of time together at the youth center. What are you guys doing out here?"

"Z brought us." Tyrone motioned to Zach.

Elam lifted a brow at Zachariah.

"When you went back, I kind of filled in for you." Zach smiled. "They wanted to see the ranch."

"He said he's gonna let us ride the horses." Mikey rubbed his hands together.

Zachariah shook his head. "*Next* time, *if* you have a permission slip."

"That's kinda why *we* stopped by. Do you mind if I take Julie for a ride?" Elam looked at Julianna to see if she was willing, then at Zach for approval.

Zach nodded. "You know the ranch is always open for you two."

"Well, we don't have too long. Our driver's supposed to pick us up at Walmart at three." He rubbed the back of his neck. "I was hoping you or Rosanna can give us a ride there around two?"

"No problem." Zach smiled. "You two have fun. You know where everything's at, so help yourselves."

"Will do." Elam turned to Julianna. "You ready to ride a horse, *Schatzi?*"

"*Jah.*" She surprised Elam by standing on her tiptoes and kissing his cheek, much to the delight of the young men present.

The moment Elam spotted the buggies in the driveway, he knew there was trouble. He recognized both of them. One belonged to Deacon Schwartz and the other one was Minister Zehr's.

What now? Elam frowned as their driver came to a stop in front of the house. Elam fished out his wallet and paid the driver.

Sure enough, he spotted the two men standing by the barn waiting.

"Why don't you take these groceries inside and put them away and I'll see what the ministers want, okay?" Elam opened the door for Julianna, then handed her the few bags that needed refrigeration. "I'll bring the rest in just a bit."

Whatever they had to say, he didn't want Julie to worry about it. He grabbed the other shopping bags and watched their driver turn out onto the main road, before meeting the men at the barn.

"Good afternoon," he greeted cordially.

"Elam." The men nodded.

Elam sighed and waited for the men to continue.

"We've heard that you have not been keeping the *Ordnung.*"

Elam frowned. "How so?"

Deacon Schwartz slipped a hand into one of his pockets and nodded once. "Visiting fence jumpers, utilizing worldly devices."

"Worldly devices? Like what?"

"A radio."

"I don't own a radio. And if you're talking about my CD player, then yes, I do own a CD player. And speakers." He blew out a breath.

Elam found abiding by the *Ordnung* to be very difficult and frustrating. He couldn't stand the bondage—having every part of his life regulated. It was much easier to submit when you thought were in danger of hell fire, but he knew that wasn't the case.

Why did they insist on making every part of life difficult? Why couldn't he own a CD player? Why couldn't he visit whomever he wanted to? Why would he use manual appliances that took at least twice as long and weren't as effective, when he could just be done with these tasks in mere minutes? It made absolutely no sense.

"So, are you saying I have to get rid of my CD player and stop visiting Zach?"

"Elam, you *are* aware of the *Ordnung*, are you not?" Deacon Schwartz asked.

He sighed. "*Jah*."

"*Gut*. Then you understand what needs to be done." The deacon nodded. "Good day."

Elam shook his head as he watched the men return to their buggies and head out of the driveway.

He moved to pet Scramble and sighed. Sometimes he wished he could be like Scramble, oblivious to everything around him. As he petted the dog, attempting to gather his thoughts before heading into the house, his father entered the barn.

"*Was is less, Sohn?*"

Elam grunted. "If I have to leave to give my wife the proper care she needs, then I will."

"Elam, you can't leave. You and Julianna have become part of the community again."

"The bishop is giving me no choice, *Daed*. I have to do what is best for Julie. If I can't provide the treatment she needs, she's not going to get better."

"What does she need?"

"It doesn't matter. It's almost as though they *want* to make things difficult for us."

"Not that long ago, you told me that you weren't looking for easy." His father met his eye. "Have you changed you mind?"

"Like I said. I'll do whatever it takes to get my wife well, whether the leadership approves of it or not."

"You are choosing a difficult path, *Sohn*."

"I don't have a choice, *Daed*." He scooped out some dog food and placed it into Scramble's dish. "The last thing Julie needs is added stress."

"And you think that being in the *Bann* and cut off from her family will not bring stress?"

"I don't know what to think anymore."

"Then pray about it, *Sohn. Der Herr* will guide you along the right path."

"I'll do that."

His father placed a hand on his shoulder. "*Gut*. I will too."

THIRTY-SIX

"Look who's here, Julie." Elam held the door open for Danny and a very pregnant Tabitha. "They came to visit before the *boppli* comes."

Julianna stared at Tabitha's middle.

"*Ach*, he's moving right now. Do you want to feel him?" Tabitha beamed as she shrugged off her coat. Danny placed it on the wall rack near the door.

Julianna looked hesitant, but Tabitha walked to where she stood near the cookstove and grasped her hand, placing it on her abdomen.

Julie's face lit up and she looked at Elam, who smiled back.

"You can feel too, Elam." Tabitha offered.

He shook his head. "No thanks."

"You will when it's your own." Danny grinned.

"That's probably a little ways off." Elam moved to stand by Julianna. "Would you two like something to drink? A snack?"

"Sure. *Denki*," Danny said.

"Go ahead and take a seat. We'll be there in a minute." Elam entered the kitchen and removed some coffee mugs from the cupboard, while Julianna poured some store-bought apple cider into a pot on the stove. He handed her the cinnamon sticks. "What did you think of the *boppli*?"

Julie shrugged and dropped the cinnamon sticks into the pot of cider along with a few other spices.

"That's pretty exciting, don't you think? We'll be an aunt and uncle soon." He smiled.

"*Jah.*" Julianna nodded and Elam wondered what she was thinking about. Perhaps they could talk more about it later after their guests left.

Elam and Julianna joined his brother and sister-in-law in the living room, handing each of them a mug of cider and a small plate of cookies.

"This place reminds me of when *Grossdawdi* and *Grossmammi* Zook visited. I miss them." Danny bit into his cookie.

"Yeah, me too." Elam sipped his cider. "That was a while ago. I'm surprised you remember."

"I think Tabitha and I might take a trip up to Ohio to visit them next year after the *boppli* is a little older. Y'all should come too."

Elam nodded and looked at Julie. "We'll have to talk about that."

"I can't tell you how glad I am to have you back in the community, Elam."

Elam smiled at his younger brother. He hadn't fully realized all he'd missed since he'd been in the *Englisch* world.

"How long you gonna be in this place for?"

"Who knows? If the sale of the house in town goes through, then we can place an offer on the property we've been looking at." Elam shrugged. "We're not really in a hurry. It's not so bad living next to *Daed* and *Mamm*. What about you guys?"

"*Ach*, still saving up money. With this *boppli* on the way...we'll see."

Elam still had a hard time picturing his baby brother as a daddy. It seemed like he was still just a *kind* himself. Responsibilities often turned boys into men.

Like each morning, Elam awakened to a star-filled sky. The absence of an alarm clock and other electric appliances made the interior of an Amish home seem even darker than usual. He'd gotten accustomed to the extra lights in the *Englisch* world, but he didn't really mind the dark.

He turned over to begin his morning ritual, which always began with kissing his wife before his feet hit the floor. Except...where was Julie?

"*Schatzi?*" he called out. He felt for the box of matches, struck a match, and lit the lantern beside the bed.

Elam grabbed his shirt and quickly buttoned it, then pulled his pants from the rack on the wall and stepped into them, pulling the suspenders up over his chest and fastening the buttons.

He looked to the hooks on Julie's side. Her dress and apron still hung there. She was most likely in the bathroom.

He walked to the bathroom and knocked, although the door wasn't completely shut. But it was dark. "You in there, *Schatzi?*"

He pushed the door open and held up the lantern. Nothing.

"Julie, where are you? Julie?" He moved to the living room and throughout the entire house calling her name. Could she be doing laundry at this hour? He checked the basement to no avail. His heartbeat quickened. *Where is she?*

He walked outside shining the light in the yard, but she was nowhere to be found. He hurried to the barn and pushed the door open. The dog came and licked his free hand.

"Scramble, have you seen Julie?" He patted his leg for the dog to follow. "Come on, boy. Help me find her."

He looked to the nearby woods and a feeling of foreboding gripped his heart. *God, where is she?*

He knocked on his folks' door, hating to wake them up at this hour. His father answered.

"*Daed*, have you seen Julie?"

"She is not with you?"

Elam shook his head. "I woke up and she was gone."

His father's eyes met his. "I'll help you look. Let me fetch the flashlight and my coat."

A brisk wind picked up sending a chill. "I'm going to grab my coat too. I'll meet you in front of the *dawdi haus*."

"Okay, *Sohn*."

A couple of moments later, they took off from the house. Elam cupped his hands and hollered, "Julie! Are you out here?"

He waited for a moment and just listened. Only silence answered back.

"Do you want to check the woods?" His father suggested.

"Let's check the road first and the phone shanty," Elam said.

"You don't think she might have gone to her folks' place?"

"At this hour? I don't know, *Daed*." He shook his head, trying to keep his wits about him. "Why would she be *anywhere* right now? She should be at home in bed."

Scramble licked Elam's hand, as though trying to reassure him. Could he feel his stress?

"I could hitch up the buggy and take a drive," *Daed* offered.

"Julie!" Elam called again. Another ominous minute ticked by, each second worse than the previous. *She has to be out here.*

"Where is she, *Daed*?" He'd found it difficult keeping the emotion out of his voice.

His father put a hand on his forearm. "It's okay, Elam. We will find her. *Der Herr* will help us."

Elam squeezed his eyes shut. *Please, God.*

Elam felt so weak. What kind of husband was he? How could he let this happen? He was supposed to be her protector, yet he couldn't even prevent her from leaving his side? He had to find her. If anything happened to her…

"Julie!"

"I'll check the shanty. Why don't you and Scramble walk toward the road, *Sohn*?"

Elam continued on without his father, constantly calling his wife's name. Still no response.

In the distance he could hear a vehicle, most likely coming around one of the curves on the mountain road. A honk rang out and he heard the car screech to a halt.

Scramble barked.

Julie!

Elam's pulse raced as he silently prayed. His heart thumped in his ears, louder with each second that passed. He ran as quickly as his legs would allow to where he thought he'd heard the commotion.

"Julie!" He called out.

"Over here. Quick!" a male voice hollered.

Elam ran up the hill to where the headlights were shining. He rounded the curve. Julie lay in the road, her white nightgown gradually turning a hue of crimson.

"I'm so sorry. I'm so sorry." The man kept saying. "I didn't see her. She was walking in the middle of the road. I slammed on my brakes. I don't think I hit her that hard."

Elam quickly knelt beside her and shrugged off his coat, then his shirt. He took his shirt, tore it into strips, and then wrapped it around the area on her leg where the blood seemed to be seeping out. He examined her body to see if any other area had been visibly injured, but found none.

He stared down at her face as she lay still. "*Schatzi?*"

Her eyes remained closed.

Elam placed his fingers along her neck, attempting to find a pulse. It beat strong and he sighed in relief. But there was no telling what kind of internal injuries she might have. He leaned down and kissed her lips, then draped his coat over her body to keep her warm.

He caressed her cheek. "Julie, can you look at me? It's Elam, your husband."

"I'll call an ambulance." The driver pulled his phone from his pocket. "I'm really sorry, man."

Daed came up the road, jogging toward them. "How is she, *Sohn?*"

"She's alive."

"We need to move her off the road. This is not safe."

Elam looked up, realizing for the first time that they were in the road. It was a good thing this road didn't see many travelers, especially at this time of day. "You're right."

"We must be very careful and keep her still."

The driver of the vehicle approached. "I can help."

Elam moved to her middle section, *Daed* to her shoulders, and the stranger to her legs.

"On the count of three. One. Two. Three." Elam nodded and they carefully lifted Julianna and carried her just beyond the road's shoulder to a soft grassy area.

A few moments later, Elam heard sirens in the distance.

Fortunately, the only injuries Julianna sustained were a fractured femur, which required surgery to insert a metal rod, and a slight concussion. The paramedic had said that it potentially could have been much worse and Elam again thanked God.

Julianna's doctor met them at the hospital and offered her advice with treatment options. It was important that Julie not receive any medications that would contraindicate any of the medications she was already on. The last thing they needed was more adverse side effects.

Elam explained the entire situation to the doctor while Julie underwent surgery.

The doctor frowned as Elam recalled the events of the morning. "Do you think this might have been a suicide attempt?"

Elam stared at the doctor. He hadn't even considered that to be a possibility. "Why would she do that?"

The doctor shrugged. "You said that she hears voices. I'm thinking that maybe the voices prompted her. The medication she's on is dangerous. I've heard some frightening stories from patients, how they've harmed themselves or others."

"She doesn't even remember doing anything. It's almost like she was sleeping the whole time. That's what scares me." Elam wove his fingers together in his lap.

"Unfortunately, that is common. They often don't realize what they are doing. Which is why it's so important to find drug-free alternatives to managing her symptoms."

"I fear we're not helping her quickly enough."

"We're doing what we can, Elam. It will take time. You've seen the progress she's made."

Elam nodded.

"What I'm looking for in Julianna's case is some kind of trigger. Did anything happen that would make her contemplate taking her life? Something out of the ordinary? She may not remember, and she may have had no intention of doing harm, but the subconscious mind can be a strong force."

"No, not that I can think of. My brother and his wife visited. They wanted to make the rounds before they have their baby."

"Have you and Julianna talked about children? Or discussed the possibility of not being able to have children?"

Elam nodded. "She knows we have to wait before we can try."

"Do you think *that* could be a motivating factor? I know having children is a big deal for the Amish."

Elam sighed. "I wouldn't think so."

"I think it would be beneficial for you and her to have a good long talk about it. Remember, part of coping is talking it out."

Relief flooded through Elam to finally have Julie home from the hospital. She hadn't stayed long, but *any* amount of time in the hospital seemed like too long in his opinion.

She wouldn't be able to do much of her exercise regimen until she fully recuperated from her surgery. Elam enlisted his mother and sister to come over and help Julianna during the day so he could work. Her mother agreed to stay with her once a week as well.

The doctor had said that they needed to discuss the childbearing issue and find out if that was indeed the cause of her sudden disappearance. The less Julie kept things bottled up inside, the better it would be for her health and wellbeing.

Elam brought his wife her morning juice. Although he needed to work, today he'd be staying home with his wife. There was a good chance that he wouldn't be able to concentrate even if he did show up at work.

He sat down next to his wife on their small sofa and draped an arm around her shoulders. "*Schatzi*, you know that we will have our own *bopplin* in *Der Herr's* time."

Tears sprung to her eyes. "But I want to give you a *boppli*, Elam. A *sohn*."

"And you will, *Gott* willing. But now isn't the time for us. We will wait for His perfect timing, *jah*?" He took her hands in his. "Listen, *Schatzi*. The most important thing right now is getting you better. If we have *kinner* now, it might not be *gut*. We don't want them to be born addicted to drugs, do we?"

"*Nee*."

"We can wait. I'm not in a hurry. We will have our *bopplin*, okay? Just not yet."

Julie nodded.

Elam moved near and placed a soft sweet kiss on her lips, holding her close. He never thought he'd be able to give this much of himself, never dreamed he could love anyone as much as he loved his wife. And the thought of losing her was unbearable.

THIRTY-SEVEN

Church had gone better than he'd expected. At first, Julianna seemed a bit confused about the *Englisch* customs. But, all in all, she seemed to enjoy sitting next to him during the service. At least, he knew that *he* enjoyed having his wife by his side.

She sang right along with the hymns she remembered from their youth gatherings, although they'd sung some of them a bit differently. And the songs she was unfamiliar with, she attempted to follow along with in the hymnal. It thrilled Elam to see the gentle smile on her face. He hoped to see many more of those in the future.

The pastor mentioned some of the same things he had spoken to Julianna about, so hopefully she understood the concept of those Scriptures a little better.

They could have a nice discussion about it when they returned home. He was looking forward to a quiet evening with his wife.

Julianna passed several doors walking through the hallway toward the restroom. She stopped. Did she just hear Elam's name? Who knows, with all the voices that usually went on inside her head? But she'd been thinking clearly today. It was a good day. Surely, she wasn't mistaken.

She stepped closer to the door that was barely open and listened.

"And that Amish girl. Is that the one Elam dumped you for?" A girl's indignant voice asked.

"I think so." Another voice said.

"I can't believe that, Megan. Really. You would beat her in a beauty contest any day, hands down."

"Don't say that. It's not nice."

"It's true. And she's overweight. What does he see in her, anyway?"

"She's not exactly fat."

The other girl laughed. "Well, she's not exactly a supermodel either."

"Who is, Chelsea? If Elam liked her enough to marry her, then I'm sure she's nice."

The other girl, Chelsea, snorted. "Yeah, because what else could it be? Seriously, Elam is hot even in that Amish getup."

"Don't talk that way. Besides, Elam has *a lot* of good qualities. He's really sweet—even when he's breaking up with you." Megan sighed.

"Which means he *should* be with you."

"We broke up. We're over." The girl reminded. "And I think he's married now."

"Well, I didn't see a ring on his finger."

"The Amish don't wear rings, silly. Come on, we better go before they lock up the building on us."

Julianna swiped at her tears and quickly slipped into the bathroom and waited until the girls were out of sight to exit through the back door. *They're right. I am fat and ugly. Elam's too good for me. He deserves someone better, someone who can give him children.*

Elam glanced over at Julianna, who looked to have been crying. He'd start a conversation with her if they were alone, but the back of Zach's SUV, with all his family present, was not the place nor the time.

He leaned over and whispered in her ear, "You okay?"

She ignored his question and stared out the window, her chin quivering.

Something was wrong. He wished they could talk about it now. Instead, he reached over and took her hand in his. He leaned over and whispered again, "It's okay. I'm here."

Elam's hands gently massaged Julianna's shoulders. He needed to coax out whatever was bothering her. "Wanna talk?"

She shook her head.

"Please, *Schatzi*. I need to know what's wrong. You can tell me."

She finally turned her eyes to his. He hated to see the sadness that dimmed them. "I…I overheard someone talking. About us."

"Where? At church?"

She nodded.

Who on earth would be talking about them at church? "What did they say?"

When she shrugged, he knew she wasn't going to be willing to share any details with him.

"Who was it?"

"Some girls." She sighed.

"Girls? Like little girls?"

"No. Some girls that know you."

Elam swallowed. "Megan?"

"I think maybe…*jah*, that was one of the names."

"And what were they saying?"

Tears began pouring down Julianna's cheeks. "Awful things, but they were true."

Elam couldn't believe what he was hearing. Who would do such a thing? "Megan said these things?"

Julianna shrugged.

Elam knelt in front of her and caressed her face, wiping away her tears with his thumbs. He caught her gaze and held it. "You listen to me, Julie. You are the most special, wonderful person I know. I love you and I don't want you to be sad, okay?"

She stared at him, her lip quivering.

"Okay, *Schatzi*?" He kissed her and asked again.

She gave one brief nod, indicating to him that she was agreeing only because it was what he wanted from her. But he knew she wasn't agreeing. *This is the last thing Julie needs.*

"Would you like to help Rosanna with dinner or would you rather rest in their spare bedroom?"

"Rest."

"Okay, *kumm*." He held out his hand to her and led the way to Zach and Rosanna's spare bedroom. He laid down next her and held her tight until he was sure she'd fallen asleep, tucked the covers around her, then carefully stepped out of the room and closed the door.

He quickly found Zach. "Hey, will you do me a favor? I need to go for a drive, it shouldn't take too long. Would you mind keeping a watch out for Julianna? She just fell asleep. If she wakes up, I'd like her to see familiar faces—especially if I'm not here."

Zach nodded. "Sure. You need to borrow my car?"

"If you don't mind."

THIRTY-EIGHT

Fury pumped through the ventricles of Elam's heart and intensified with every step toward Megan's house. He reined in a frustrated breath and attempted to gather his wits about him before he busted the door down. He did his best to knock calmly but he wasn't feeling it at all.

"Elam?" The door opened and Megan stood in front of him, but right now he couldn't stand to look at her. Right now, all he could see was Julianna's tears. "What are you doing he—"

"What did you and your friend say about my wife?" He couldn't help his raised voice or his flaring anger.

"What are you talking about?"

His hands fisted at his side. "At church. You and someone else were talking."

Her countenance immediately changed and the color seemed to drain from her face. She frowned. "Your wife heard our conversation?"

"What did you say?" He enunciated each syllable.

"Elam...if I had any idea she was...I'm sorry."

His arms crossed firmly over his solid chest.

"It was Chelsea. She just speaks her mind. She said some things that I'm sure would be hurtful."

He tapped his foot, growing more impatient by the second.

Megan continued. "She said that she didn't know what you saw in Julianna. She didn't understand why you would choose someone who was overweight and not very pretty. That you would choose her over me."

His heart squeezed tight. He wished with everything in him that Julianna hadn't heard those things spoken about her. But it was too late. Spoken words may be forgiven, they may eventually be forgotten, but they could never ever be taken back.

Megan didn't need to know that the reason for Julianna's current weight was because of the medication she was taking. Besides that, he loved her anyway. And he would continue to love her whether she ever lost the weight or not. Because, unlike some people, he knew a person's value wasn't measured by how much they weighed or how beautiful they were on the outside. One's worth came from the Creator, and each individual was precious in His sight. And to Elam, Julianna was beautiful. He just wished she was healthy.

"Hurtful? Those things are more than just hurtful, Megan. To my wife, those words are life-threatening! She's very fragile. She's already tried to take her life once!" He knew he was yelling but he couldn't help it. This would no doubt set Julie back who knew how far. "I've tried *so* hard to get her where she was and you destroyed all of that in one conversation!"

"I'm sorry, Elam, but I can't control what comes out of other people's mouths. Chelsea isn't saved."

"Maybe not. But *you* stood there and listened, didn't you?"

Megan hung her head.

"Out of all places, I thought that church would be the one safe place I could bring her to and not have to worry about or deal with anything negative. And now this." Words could not express how disappointed Elam was with Megan right now.

"I can apologize to her if you think it would help."

He shook his head and quickly dismissed her. "No, the damage has already been done, and that might just humiliate her even more."

"I don't know what you want from me, Elam. What can I do to make this better?"

He sighed. "You can pray that she doesn't do anything harmful." He turned to walk back to Zach's vehicle.

"I'm sorry, Elam."

He heard Megan's words but he was too upset to acknowledge them. He needed to get back before Julianna woke up and discovered he wasn't there. The last thing she needed was a panic attack.

He cursed the air in frustration. He'd thought that bringing her to church today would be a good, positive step in the right direction. How wrong he'd been.

Elam took a calming breath and attempted to rein in his thoughts, to get rid of this stress. He would be no good to Julianna if he was emanating negative emotions. *God, I'm stressed out here. I need Your help. Please see me and Julie through this. Give me the strength I need to be who Julie needs. I can't do this on my own. Denki. Amen.*

Elam approached the house and spotted Zach outside with two of his children throwing a baseball back and forth. It reminded Elam of his youth days, when their Amish group would meet together and play softball, usually before a singing. Those were good times—carefree times that he longed for again. Would he and Julie ever know days like that? Would there ever be a time when he wouldn't worry about her hurting herself or someone else?

"Is Julie up?"

"No. Rosanna's in the kitchen. I told her to let me know if Julianna awakens."

"Okay, thanks." Elam lifted the keys and Zach motioned for him to toss them to him.

Elam headed to the bedroom as soon as he stepped inside the house. He opened the door to find Julie still safely sleeping and breathed a sigh of relief. Oh, how he loved her and longed for her to be free of the burdens she carried. If she could just give them to God…

"Elam?" Julie sat up.

He quickly went to her. "You okay, *Schatzi*? Did you have a good nap?"

"*Jah.*"

He sat down next to her a tucked a strand of hair behind her ear. "I talked to Megan. She told me what happened, what her friend said. I didn't think those were very kind things to say."

"But they were true. Maybe you should have married Megan." She stared down at her hands.

He gently lifted her chin and waited until her eyes met his. "No, they weren't true. And I didn't marry Megan because I didn't love her."

A single tear slid down her cheek. No doubt, she'd been consumed by feelings of self-deprecation. Who wouldn't after overhearing a conversation like that?

Elam took her in his arms and pulled her close to him. He gazed into her forlorn eyes. He gentled his tone. "Want to know a secret?"

His eyes searched hers and she nodded slightly.

"It's a well-kept secret that I'd hidden deep inside my soul. I love you. I've always loved you. I tried to forget you, to make myself stop loving you, but my heart just wouldn't listen. There's only one person I can ever love for all my life—and that's you. Not Megan or any other girl. I. Love. *You*. Julianna."

He didn't wait for her response. Instead, he lowered his lips onto hers, proving his words the best he knew how. She seemed hesitant at first, but eventually surrendered to his advances.

He broke away. "You need not *ever* doubt my love for you, sweet Julie." Then he continued the kiss he wished would never stop.

THIRTY-NINE

Elam stood in front of the pew, with Julianna by his side, singing hymns of joy to His magnificent Saviour. He thought of God and His goodness, His mercy, His love, and couldn't keep the smile off his face.

If it weren't for a few off days here and there, their struggles of the recent past could almost be forgotten. *Almost.* Elam was confident that he and Julianna had been given a new lease on life. Of course, everyone had bad days, he knew that. But somehow, it seemed that even the bad days were a blessing because they reminded him and made him thankful for all the good days. He'd once heard it said that bad times are there to remind us to be thankful for the good times.

Very few signs remained of the struggles they endured over the past year and a half. In fact, they both felt happier and healthier than they'd ever been. The doctor insisted it was mostly the diet, which Elam couldn't deny played a big part. But he knew it was more than that. It was being a part of a wonderful Amish community and having friends like Zach and Rosanna nearby. It was the joy and love they shared each day in each other's presence. It was the blessings of *Der Herr* which continually surrounded them.

It seemed since Julie had placed her trust in Christ, she'd learned to give her doubts and fears over to Him. She'd allowed Him to fill her with His peace, His joy.

Daed had gone to the ministers awhile back and reasoned with them. Somehow, he'd convinced them to make an exception for the 'contraband' Elam and Julianna needed— for the greater good of the community, of course.

Things weren't perfect, by any means. Elam still found himself in conflict with the leaders. There were just some things he refused to compromise on. He and Julianna occasionally visited his former *Englisch* church, but they also faithfully attended every other Sunday in their Amish district. So far, they'd been able to avoid the *Bann.*

It seemed that Julianna enjoyed their *Englisch* church as much as Elam did. Perhaps it helped that Megan had been away on a mission's trip over the last year. Although he'd been upset with Megan the last time they'd spoken, he hadn't held a grudge. People would always be people. And people would say things. That was life. He had felt bad about not apologizing, though. That was something he'd planned to set right today.

As soon as the service was over, Elam searched the auditorium until he spotted Megan.

He turned to his wife. "Do you want to go with me to talk to Megan or would you rather stay here with Zach and Rosanna?"

Julie smiled. "You go. I'll be here. But don't be long because we're supposed to barbeque out at the ranch today, remember? Veggie burgers." She raised her eyebrows twice in quick succession and winked.

He leaned over and kissed her cheek. "That's right. I shouldn't be more than a few minutes."

Elam approached Megan toward the back of the sanctuary. "Hey, can we talk?"

Megan shrugged. "Sure."

Elam blew out a breath. Apologizing had never been the easiest thing for him to do. "I'm sorry for the harsh words I spoke to you that last time we talked. I was really upset and concerned about my wife. I know that it wasn't your fault, but I took out my anger on you. Please, forgive me."

Megan nodded. "I know why you said those things. I didn't blame you at all. I just felt bad about the whole thing. How is your wife doing now?"

"Better every day. The doctor said she is doing very well."

"I'm happy to hear that. She looks great." Megan smiled. "You know, what you've done for her is admirable."

Elam shook his head. "I've just shown her love that every human being deserves."

"No, I think you've gone above and beyond that."

Chase walked up behind Megan. "Hey, Elam. It seems

like I haven't seen you in forever. What's up?" He reached for Megan's hand and their fingers intertwined.

"You know I went back to the Amish."

Chase nodded. "And I heard you got married."

"Yeah, that was a while back. Over a year ago." Elam nodded.

"Well, you're not the only one with good news." Chase beamed down at Megan and winked. "I've asked Megan to marry me and she said yes!"

"Really?" He looked to both of them and they both nodded and smiled. "That's wonderful. Congratulations."

"Thanks. Will you and your wife be able to attend our wedding or is that like against Amish policies?"

Elam chuckled. "No, we're allowed to attend *Englisch* weddings. I'll talk to Julie about it and see if she's up to going. When is it?"

Chase grinned. "We're not quite sure yet, but we'll send you an invitation when we get to that stage in the planning process."

"That sounds *gut*." Elam watched as his two friends walked off. Who would have thought Chase and Megan would end up together? Certainly not him. He now wondered if Chase had liked Megan all along, and if so, why he hadn't asked her out before Elam had? Not that any of that mattered now. The past was past.

He looked back toward the pew he'd shared with Julie earlier and found her talking to one of the ladies of the church. She was so beautiful and full of life. Every day he thanked God for giving them a second chance. He caught her eye and winked, then made his way toward her.

EPILOGUE

Two Years Later…

Elam startled awake and immediately shot up. He looked to Julianna's side of the bed. Empty. *No. Lord, please.* The last time this had occurred he'd found Julie in the middle of the road, nearly dead.

He jumped up, not even bothering to grab his broadfalls or shirt. "Julianna?" He hollered.

Nothing.

He paused for a moment and covered his face with both of his hands. *Dear God, if You can hear me, please be with Julie wherever she is. Please keep her safe.*

He grabbed his coat and threw it on and hastily slipped his boots on. His heart pounded with each step.

"Julie?" He cupped his hands and called out into the wooded area behind the house. This felt eerily similar to last time and Elam could not shake the dread that had taken hold of him, clenched down on his heart. He attempted to calm himself. *Julie should be fine now. She hasn't had an episode in over a year.*

"Elam?"

He spun around. His beautiful wife stood at the door of their home. *She's safe!* He wanted to sink to the ground and weep.

"*Schatzi?* You're alright?"

Julianna smiled. "I'm fine." She eyed him from top to bottom. "What are you doing outside in your boxer shorts?"

"Looking for you."

"You better hope the bishop doesn't stop by, otherwise he's going to commit *you* to a mental institution."

She was teasing.

Elam wanted to burst into laughter, the joy of seeing her alive and well felt so good. He looked down at his attire. Boxers, boots, and a coat. "*Jah*, I guess I do look pretty silly."

Julianna giggled. "Yes, you do. Come inside."

He stepped into the house and took her into his arms. "Where were you?"

"In the bathroom."

He pulled back. "But I called and you didn't answer me." He quickly shrugged out of his coat and removed his boots.

"I was sick, Elam. I couldn't really respond right then." She stared into his eyes.

"Sick? What kind of sick?"

She rubbed her stomach.

He frowned. The last thing Julie needed was sickness.

Perhaps her body was detoxing out more of the poisons.

"It was the third time it's happened this week, but only the first time you woke up."

"The third time? But you...? Wait." His eyes flew wide and he took in his wife's expression. "You're...you're in the family way?"

She smiled and nodded.

"Oh, *Schatzi*. But how? I thought–"

"You thought wrong. *Der Herr* has blessed you with a little arrow."

A smile stretched across his face, easing more of the tension he previously felt. "Do you think we might get a quiver full of arrows?"

"I'm hoping only one or two at a time."

"Two?" His brow shot up.

She shrugged. "My mother was a twin. I heard that it could run in the family."

"You still feeling bad? I can make you some tea," he offered, moving close to the woodstove.

"No, I'm better now. But *denki* for offering." She yawned. "I think I might want to just go back to bed and sleep a little longer." She placed her hands on his chest and raised a brow. "How about you, handsome?"

Fire burned in his chest where her touch had branded and he gazed into her eyes. His heart rate quickened. He lifted her into his arms and caressed her cheek, melding his lips to hers. "Yes, sleep sounds wonderful."

The End

Thanks for reading!

To find out more about J.E.B. Spredemann, join our email list, or purchase other books, please visit us at www.jebspredemann.com. Our books are available in Paperback, eBook, and Audiobook formats. You can find them at your favorite book store or library (if you don't see it on the shelf at either of these places, just ask) or at your preferred online retailer.

To GOD be the glory!

A SPECIAL THANK YOU

I'd like to take this time to thank everyone that had any involvement in this book and its production, including Mom and Dad, who have always been supportive of my writing, my longsuffering Family - especially my handsome, encouraging Hubby, my former-Amish friends who have helped immensely in my understanding of the Amish ways, my supportive Pastor and Church family, my Proofreaders, my Editor, my CIA Facebook friends who have been a tremendous help, my wonderful Readers who buy, read, and leave encouraging reviews and emails, my awesome Street Team who, I'm confident, will 'Sprede the Word' about my books! And last, but certainly not least, I'd like to thank my Precious LORD and SAVIOUR JESUS CHRIST, for without Him, none of this would have been possible!

A Secret Sacrifice Discussion Questions
Potential Spoilers

1. At the onset of the story, Elam is pretty content, yet feels like something is lacking in his life. Have you ever felt this way?

2. Tragedy happens all around us every day. We often read or hear of news stories featuring accidents involving Amish buggies. If you've ever driven in Amish country, have you feared running into a buggy?

3. Elam, the hero in the story, was first mentioned in *An Undeniable Secret*—book four in the *Amish Secrets* series. If you've read that book, did you like his character then?

4. When Elam first learns of Julianna's presumed fate, he is devastated inside but has to hide his emotions. Have you ever been in a similar predicament?

5. Elam and Zach are not only cousins but good friends. Have you ever experienced this type of relationship with a close relative?

6. In an attempt to move on and forget about his heartbreak, Elam considers dating again although he has no clue as

to how *Englischers* do dating. Have you ever been in an awkward situation totally out of your cultural norm?

7. Do you think a lasting relationship between Elam and Megan could work? Why or why not?

8. Sometimes tragedies can be a catalyst in our lives to finding Christ. This was true for Danny. Have you ever experienced the joy and excitement of leading someone to Christ?

9. When Elam discovers the truth regarding Julianna, he feels duty-bound (and perhaps love-bound) to help, in spite of probable negative consequences. Do you think he made the right decision? What do you think you would have done, given the same situation?

10. Even though Elam knew it would take faith and endurance to care for Julie, he chose to do so because she needed him. According to God's Word, do you think he did the right thing? Why or why not?

11. This book opens up the topic of the dangers of psychotropic medications. Were you aware of those dangers prior to reading this book?

12. Have you ever used a natural method of healing (such as juicing) as opposed to pharmaceutical medication?

13. Caring for a loved one with a sickness can be difficult and emotionally draining at times. Have you ever cared for a loved one with a mental sickness or addiction? How did you cope with your own mental health during that time?

14. Another topic this book mentions is gossip. People tend to say things to others when they think nobody else is around. As we've seen from the situation in the church scene, the consequences of something we think is harmless can, indeed, be very harmful. Being in Megan's shoes, how would you have responded to Chelsea's words? Was there something more Megan could have done?

15. Do you feel like this book drew you closer to God? Why or why not?

16. Do you have a favorite quote or scene from the book? Please share.

BOOKS IN THIS SERIES INCLUDE:

Have you read the *Amish by Accident* trilogy? Here's a sneak peek at book One in the series, *Englisch on Purpose.*

CHAPTER ONE

Matthew listened closely. Did he hear something? He peeked over at Maryanna in the darkness, who lay by his side, softly snoring.

A soft click told him all he needed to know. He hastily rose from the bed and pulled his suspendered pants on quietly. He nearly tumbled over his work boots as he tiptoed toward the living room. He flipped the lights on.

"Dad?" His daughter's surprised expression was wrought with anguish.

His muscled forearms crossed his chest. "What are you doing out at this hour? Your curfew was an hour ago, young lady." He pointed to the clock on the wall.

"I…I…uh, Johnny and Judah wanted to stay out longer. I told them I had to be home."

"That's not good enough. Try again." He raised a brow.

"What's going on?" Matthew turned at Maryanna's voice.

"Our daughter is *just now* returning home."

"Matthew, can't we discuss this in the morning? I'm sure Mattie's tired."

Matthew didn't miss the 'thanks, Mom' look Mattie tossed Maryanna. "I think it needs to be discussed now," he insisted.

"Why?" Maryanna challenged him.

"Why? Because this is important, that's why. And by the time she awakens in the morning, I'll have been working a couple of hours. At least."

Their daughter, Rebekah, walked into the kitchen, yawning. "What's going on, Mom?"

"Your sister, here, is late. Once again." Matthew frowned. "You may go back to bed, Rebekah."

Mattie's hands flew up. "I don't know what you want me to say, Dad. I've told you the truth." She yawned. "I'm tired. Can I go to bed now?"

"No." He held out his hand. "Give me your keys."

"But, Dad–"

"Now." Matthew tempered his frustration as best as he could.

Tears welled in his daughter's eyes and she yanked her car keys from her purse.

Matthew clenched his fingers around them. "You're grounded for two weeks."

"But how will I get to school and work without my car?"

"Perhaps you should have thought about that *before* you decided to return home late."

"Matthew, isn't this a little harsh?" Maryanna's hand caressed his back.

Matthew frowned. "No, this is not harsh. We've been over this before. She's had fair warning. She needs to realize there are consequences for her actions." He turned back to their daughter. "Go to bed, Mattie."

"You're just like *Dawdi* Sabastian!"

He grimaced as his daughter flew up the stairs in tears. Being compared to his ultra-strict Amish father was not a compliment by any stretch of the word.

"Are you sure that was the best thing to do?"

Matthew stared at his wife in disbelief. "Listen, Maryanna. I need you to support me. We need to be in agreement."

"I just don't think that was the best thing to do."

"And what would *you* have done?"

"I probably would have waited until tomorrow, then I would have reasoned with her."

"We've tried that already, remember?" Matthew sighed. "Maryanna, do you think it's easy for me to put restrictions on our children? Well, it's not. She knows better. And Mattie staying out late is asking for trouble. Especially if she's with Jonathan's boys."

Maryanna exhaled. "You have a point."

"Okay, Lis, I've had it! My parents are driving me crazy," Mattie ranted. "If they keep this up, I think I'm going to scream."

Elisabeth eyed her best friend. "I can't believe they took your car away."

"Not the car, just the keys. Which is essentially the same thing, I guess." Mattie paced from Elisabeth's bedroom window to her desk, then plopped down in her chair. "I'm thinking of leaving."

"Mattie, don't leave. What am I going to do if you're gone?"

"Come with me then."

"I don't know. It's kind of scary." Elisabeth shook her head. "Where will you go? Who will you stay with?"

"I'm sure I'll find a place. I've been saving up money from my job." Mattie tapped her chin. "I think I'll look up 'Help Wanted' ads in New York."

Elisabeth's eyes widened. "New York?"

"I've always wanted to go there. Why not?"

"But it's so big. And there are *ferhoodled* people there."

Mattie smiled at her Amish best friend. "There are *ferhoodled* people everywhere, Lis. Just look at my cousins." She laughed, thinking of Johnny and Judah and all the mischief the twins had gotten into over the years...

Find **Englisch on Purpose** at your favorite online retailer or request for purchase at your favorite bookstore or local library.

CPSIA information can be obtained
at www.ICGtesting.com
Printed in the USA
LVHW042307310720
662090LV00005B/621

9 781940 492308